CHARLES STROSS

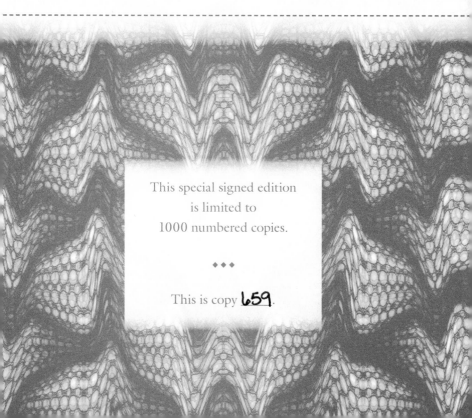

This special signed edition
is limited to
1000 numbered copies.

◆◆◆

This is copy **659**.

PALIMPSEST

PALIMPSEST

CHARLES STROSS

Illustrated by J. K. Potter

Subterranean Press 2011

First Edition

ISBN
978-1-59606-421-8

Subterranean Press
PO Box 190106
Burton, MI 48519

www.subterraneanpress.com

FRESH MEAT

THIS WILL NEVER HAPPEN:

You will flex your fingers as you stare at the back of the youth you are going to kill, father to the man who will never now become your grandfather; and as you trail him home through the snowy night, you'll pray for your soul, alone in the darkness.

Memories are going to come to you unbidden even though you'll try to focus on the task in hand. His life—that part of it which you arrived kicking and squalling in time to share with him before the end—will pass in front of your eyes. You will remember Gramps in his sixties, his hands a bunch of raisin-wrinkled grape joints as he holds your preteen wrists and shows you how to cast the fly across the water. And you'll remember the shrunken husk of his seventies, standing speechless and numb by Gran's graveside in his too-big suit, lying at last alone in the hospice bed, breath coming shallow and fast as he sleeps alone with the cancer. These won't be good memories. But you know the rest of the story too, having heard it endlessly from your parents: young love and military service in a war as distant as faded sepia photographs from another generation's front, a good job in the factory and a wife he will quietly adore who will in due course give him three children, from one of whose loins you in turn are drawn. Gramps will have a good, long life and live to see five grandchildren and a myriad of wonders, and this boy-man on the edge of adulthood who you are compelled to follow as he walks to the recruiting office holds the seeds of the man you will remember... But it's him or you.

Gramps would have had a good life. You must hold on to that. It will make what's coming easier.

You will track the youth who will never be your grandfather through the snow-spattered shrubbery and long grass along the side of the railroad tracks, and the wool-and-vegetable-fiber cloth that you wear—your costume will be entirely authentic—chafes your skin. By that point you won't have bathed for a week, or shaved using hot water: you are a young thug, a vagrant, and a wholly bad sort. That is what the witnesses will see, the mad-eyed young killer in the sweat-stained suit with the knife and his victim, so vulnerable with his throat laid open almost to the bone. He'll sprawl as if he is merely sleeping. And there will be outrage and alarm as the cops and concerned citizens turn out to hunt the monster that took young Gerry from his family's arms, and him just barely a man: but they won't find you, because you'll push the button on the pebble-sized box and Stasis Control will open up a timegate and welcome you into their proud and lonely ranks.

When you wake up in your dorm two hundred years-objective from now, bathed in stinking fear-sweat, with the sheet sucking onto your skin like a death-chilled caul, there will be nobody to comfort you and nobody to hold you. The kindness of your mother's hands and the strength of your father's wrists will be phantoms of memory, ghosts that echo round your bones, wandering homeless through the mausoleum of your memories.

They'll have no one to remember their lives but you; and all because you will believe the recruiters when they tell you that to join the organization you must kill your own grandfather, and that if you do not join the organization, you will die.

(It's an antinepotism measure, they'll tell you, nodding, not unkindly. And a test of your ruthlessness and determination. And besides, we all did it when it was *our* turn.)

Welcome to the Stasis, Agent Pierce! You're rootless now, an orphan of the time stream, sprung from nowhere on a mission to eternity. And you're going to have a *remarkable* career.

YELLOWSTONE

"You've got to remember, humanity always goes extinct," said Wei, staring disinterestedly at the line of women and children shuffling toward the slave station down by the river. "*Always.* A thousand years, a hundred thousand, a quarter million—doesn't matter. Sooner or later, humans go extinct." He was speaking Urem, the language the Stasis used among themselves.

"I thought that was why we were here? To try and prevent it?" Pierce asked, using the honorific form appropriate for a student questioning his tutor, although Wei was, in truth, merely a twelfth-year trainee himself: the required formality was merely one more reminder of the long road ahead of him.

"No." Wei raised his spear and thumped its base on the dry, hard-packed mud of the observation mound. "We're going to relocate a few seed groups, several tens of thousands. But the rest are still going to die." He glanced away from the slaves: Pierce followed his gaze.

Along the horizon, the bright red sky darkened to the color of coagulated blood on a slaughterhouse floor. The volcano, two thousand kilometers farther around the curve of the planet, had been pumping ash and steam into the stratosphere for weeks. Every noon, in the badlands where once the Mississippi delta had writhed, the sky wept brackish tears.

"You're from before the first extinction epoch, aren't you? The pattern wasn't established back then. That must be why you were sent on this field trip. You need to understand that this *always* happens. Why we do this. You need to know it in your guts. Why we take the savages and leave the civilized to die."

Like Wei, and the other Stasis agents who had silently liquidated the camp guards and stolen their identities three nights before, Pierce was disguised as a Benzin warrior. He wore the war paint and beaten-aluminum armbands, bore the combat scars. He carried a spear tipped with a shard of synthetic diamond, mined from a deep seam of prehistoric automobile windshields. He even wore a Benzin face: the epicanthic folds and dark skin conferred by the phenotypic patches had given him food for thought, an unfamiliar departure from his white-bread origins. Gramps (he shied from the memory) would have died rather than wear this face.

Pierce was not yet even a twelve-year trainee: he'd been in the service for barely four years-subjective. But he was ready to be sent out under supervision, and this particular operation called for warm bodies rather than retrocausal subtlety.

Fifty years ago, the Benzin had swept around the eastern coastline of what was still North America, erupting from their heartland in the central isthmus to extend their tribute empire into the scattered tribal grounds of post-Neolithic nomads known to Stasis Control only by their code names: the Alabamae, the

Floridae, and the Americae. The Benzin were intent on conquering the New World, unaware that it had been done at least seventeen times already since the start of the current Reseeding. They did not understand the significance of the redness in the western sky or the shaking of the ground, ascribing it to the anger of their tribal gods. They had no idea that these signs heralded the end of the current interglacial age, or that their extinction would be a side effect of the coming Yellowstone eruption—one of a series that occurred at six-hundred-thousand-year intervals during the early stages of the Lower First Anthropogenic epoch.

The Benzin didn't take a long view of things, for although their priest-kings had a system of writing, most of them lived in the hazily defined ahistorical myth-world of the preliterate. Their time was running out all the same. Yellowstone was waking, and even the Stasis preferred to work around such brutal geological phenomena, rather than through them.

"Yes, but why take *them?*" Pierce nodded toward the silently trudging Alabamae women and children, their shoulders stooped beneath the burden of their terror. They'd been walking before the spear points of their captors for days; they were exhausted. The loud ones had already died, along with the lame. The raiders who had slain their men and stolen them away to a life of slavery sat proudly astride their camels, their enemies' scalps dangling from their kotekas like bizarre pubic wigs. "The Benzin may be savages, but these people are losers—they came off worse."

Wei shook his head minutely. "The adults are all female, and mostly pregnant at that. These are the healthy ones, the ones who survived the march. They're gatherers, used to living off the land, and they're all in one convenient spot."

Pierce clenched his teeth, realizing his mistake. "You're going to use them for Reseeding? Because there are fewer bodies, and they're more primitive, more able to survive in a wilderness...?"

"Yes. For a successful Reseeding we need at least twenty thousand bodies from as many diverse groups as possible, and even then we risk a genetic bottleneck. And they need to be able to survive in the total absence of civilization. If we dumped *you* in the middle of a Reseeding, you would probably not last a month. No criticism intended; neither would I. Those warriors"—Wei raised his spear again, as if saluting the raiders—"require slaves and womenfolk and a hierarchy to function. The tip of your spear was fashioned by a slave in the royal armories, not by a warrior. Your moccasins and the cloth of your pants were made by Benzin slaves. They are halfway to reinventing civilization: given another five thousand years-subjunctive, their distant descendants might build steam engines and establish ubiquitous recording frameworks, bequeathing their memories to the absolute future. But for a Reseeding they're as useless as we are."

"But they don't have half a deci—"

"Be still. They're moving."

13

The last of the slaves had been herded between the barbed hedges of the entrance passageway, and the gate guards lifted the heavy barrier back into position. Now the raiders kicked their mounts into motion, beating and poking them around the side of the spiny bamboo fence in a circuit of the guard posts. Wei and Pierce stood impassively as the camel riders spurred down on them. At the last moment, their leader pulled sideways, and his mount snorted and pawed at the ground angrily as he leaned toward Wei.

"Hai!" he shouted, in the tonal trade tongue of the northern Benzin. "I don't remember you!"

"I am Hawk! Who in the seventh hell are *you*?"

Wei glared at the rider, but the intruder just laughed raucously and spat over the side of his saddle: it landed on the mud, sufficiently far from Wei to make it unclear whether it was a direct challenge.

Pierce tightened his grip on his spear, moving his index finger closer to the trigger discreetly printed on it. High above them, a vulturelike bird circled the zone of confrontation with unnatural precision, its fire-control systems locked on.

"I am Teuch," said the rider, after a pause. "I captured these women! In the name of our Father I took them, and in the name of our Father I got them with children to work in the paddies! What have you done for our Father today?"

"I stand here," Wei said, lifting the butt of his spear. "I guard our Father's flock while assholes like you are out having fun."

"Hai!" The rider's face split in a broad, dust-stained grin. "I see you, too!" He raised his right fist and for an instant Pierce had an icy vision of his guts unraveling around a barbarian's spear; but the camel lifted its head and brayed as Teuch nudged it in a surprisingly delicate sidestep away from Wei, away from the hedge of thorns, away from the slave station. And away from the site of the timegate through which the evacuation team would drive the camp inmates in two days' time. The prisoners would be deposited at the start of the next Reseeding. But none of the Benzin would live to see that day, a hundred thousand years-objective or more in the future.

Perhaps their camels would leave their footprints in the choking, hot rain of ash that would roll across the continent with tomorrow's sunset. Perhaps some of those footprints would fossilize, so that the descendants of the Alabamae slaves would uncover them and marvel at their antiquity in the age to come. But immortality, Pierce thought, was a poor substitute for not dying.

Paying Attention in Class

IT WAS A BRIGHT and chilly day on the roof of the world. Pierce, his bare head shaved like the rest of the green-robed trainees, sat on a low stool in a courtyard beneath the open sky, waiting for the tutorial to begin.

Riding high above the ancient stone causeway and the spiral minarets of the Library Annex, the moon bared her knife-slashed cheeks at Pierce, as if to remind him of how far he'd come.

"Good afternoon, Honorable Students."

The training camp nestled in a valley among the lower peaks of the Mediterranean Alps. Looming over the verdant lowlands of the Sahara basin, in this epoch they rose higher than the stumps of the time-weathered Himalayas.

"Good afternoon, Honorable Scholar Yarrow," chanted the dozen students of the sixth-year class.

Urem, like Japanese before it, paid considerable attention to the relative status of speaker and audience. Many of the cultures the Stasis interacted with were sensitive to matters of gender, caste, and other signifiers of rank, so the designers of Urem had added declensions to reflect these matters. New recruits were expected to practice the formalities diligently, for a mastery of Urem was important to their future—and none of them were native speakers.

"I speak to you today of the structure of human history and the ways in which we may interact with it."

Yarrow, the Honorable Scholar, was of indeterminate age: robed in black, her hair a stubble-short golden halo, she could have been anywhere from thirty to three hundred. Given the epigenetic overhaul the Stasis provided for their own, the latter was likelier—but not three thousand. Attrition in the line of duty took its toll over the centuries. Yarrow's gaze, when it fell on Pierce, was clear, her eyes the same blue as the distant horizon. This was the first time she had lectured Pierce's class—not surprising, for the college had many tutors, and the path to graduation was long enough to tax the most disciplined. She was, he understood, an expert on what was termed the Big Picture. He hadn't looked her up in the local Library Annex ahead of time. (In his experience it was generally better to approach these lessons with an open mind. And in any case, students had only patchy access to the records of their seniors.)

"As a species, we are highly unstable, prone to Malthusian crises and self-destructive wars. This apparent weakness is also our strength—when reduced to a rump of a few thousand illiterate hunter-gatherers, we can spread out and tame a planet in mere centuries, and build high civilizations in a handful of millennia.

"Let me give you some numbers. Over the two and a half million epochs accessible to us—each of which lasts for a million years—we shall have reseeded starter populations nearly twenty-one million times, with an average extinction period of sixty-nine thousand years. Each Reseeding event produces an average of eleven-point-six planet-spanning empires, thirty-two continental empires, nine hundred and sixty-odd languages spoken by more than one million people, and a total population of one-point-seven trillion individuals. Summed over the entire life span of this planet—which has been vastly extended by the cosmological engineering program you see above you every night—there are nearly twenty billion billion of us. We are not merely legion—we rival in our numbers the stars of the observable universe in the current epoch.

"Our species is legion. And throughout the vast span of our history, ever since the beginning of the first panopticon empire during our first flowering, we have committed to permanent storage a record of everything that has touched us—everything but those events that have definitively unhappened."

Pierce focused on Yarrow's lips. They quirked slightly as she spoke, as if the flavor of her words was bitter—or as if she was suppressing an unbidden humor, intent on maintaining her gravitas before the class. Her mouth was wide and sensual, and her lips curiously pale, as if they were waiting to be warmed by another's touch. Despite his training, Pierce was as easily distracted as any other twentysomething male, and try as he might, he found it difficult to focus on her words: he came from an age of hypertext and canned presentations and found that these archaic, linear tutorials challenged his concentration. The outward austerity of her delivery inflamed his imagination, blossoming in a sensuous daydream in which the wry taste of her lips blended with the measured cadences of her speech to burn like fire in his mind.

"Uncontrolled civilization is a terminal consumptive state, as the victims of the first extinction discovered the hard way. We have left their history intact and untouched, that we might remember our origins and study them as a warning; some of you in this cohort have been recruited from that era. In other epochs we work to prevent wild efflorescences of resource-depleting overindustrialization, to suppress competing abhuman intelligences, and to prevent the pointless resource drain of attempts to colonize other star systems. By shepherding this planet's resources and manipulating its star and neighboring planets to maximize its inhabitable duration, we can achieve Stasis—a system that supports human life for a thousand times the life of the unmodified sun, and that remembers the time line of every human life that ever happened."

Yarrow's facts and figures slid past Pierce's attention like warm syrup. He paid little heed to them, focusing instead on her intonation, the little twitches of the muscles in her cheeks as she framed each word, the rise and fall of her chest as she breathed in and out. She was impossibly magnetic: a puritan sex icon, ascetic and unaware, attractive but untouchable. It was foolish in the extreme, he knew, but for some combination of tiny interlocking reasons he found her unaccountably exciting.

"All of this would be impossible without our continued ownership of the timegate. You already know the essentials. What you may not be aware of is that it is a unique, easily depleted resource. The timegate allows us to open wormholes connecting two openings in four-dimensional space-time. But the exclusion principle prevents two such openings from overlapping in time. Tear-up and tear-down is on the order of seven milliseconds, a seemingly tiny increment when you compare it to the trillion-year span that falls within our custody. But when you slice a period of interest into fourteen-millisecond chunks, you run out of time fast. Each such span can only ever be touched by us once, connected to one other place and time of our choosing.

"Stasis Control thus has access to a theoretical maximum of 5.6 times 10^{21} slots across the totality of our history—but our legion of humanity comes perilously close, with a total of 2 times 10^{19} people. Many of the total available slots are reserved for data, relaying the totality of recorded human history to the Library—fully ninety-six percent of humanity lives in eras where ubiquitous surveillance or personal life-logging technologies have made the recording of absolute history possible, and we obviously need to archive their lifelines. Only the ur-historical prelude to Stasis, and periods of complete civilizational collapse and Reseeding, are not being monitored in exhaustive detail.

"To make matters worse: in practice there are far fewer slots available for actual traffic, because we are not, as a species, well equipped for reacting in spans of less than a second. The seven-millisecond latency of a timegate is shorter by an order of magnitude than the usual duration of a gate used for transport.

"We dare not use gates for iterated computational processes, or to open permanent synchronous links between epochs, and while we could in theory use it to enable a single faster-than-light starship, that would be horribly wasteful. So we are limited to blink-and-it's-gone wormholes connecting time slices of interest. And we must conclude that the slots we allocate to temporal traffic are a scarce resource because—"

Yarrow paused and glanced across her audience. Pierce shifted slightly on his stool, a growing tension in his crotch giving his distraction a focus. Her gaze lingered on him a moment too long, as if she sensed his inattention: the slight hint of amusement, imperceptible microexpressions barely glimpsed at the corners of her mouth, sent a panicky shiver up his spine. *She's going to ask questions,* he realized, as she opened her lips. "What applications of the timegate are ruled out by the slot latency period, class? Does anyone know? Student Pierce? What do *you* know?" She looked at him directly, expectantly. The half smile nibbled at her cheeks, but her eyes were cool.

"I, um, I don't—" Pierce flailed for words, dragged back to the embarrassing present from his sensual daydream. "The latency period?"

"You don't *what?*" Honorable Scholar Yarrow raised one perfect eyebrow in feigned disbelief at his fluster. "But of course, Student Pierce. You *don't.* That has always been your besetting weakness: you're easily distracted. Too curious for your own good." Her smile finally broke, icy amusement crinkling around her eyes. "See me in my office after the tutorial," she said, then turned her attention back to the rest of the class, leaving him to stew in fearful anticipation. "I do hope you have been paying more attention—"

The rest of Yarrow's lecture slid past Pierce in a delirium of embarrassment as she spoke of deep time, of salami-sliced vistas of continental drift and re-formation, of megayears devoted to starlifting and the frozen, lifeless gigayears during which the Earth had been dislodged from its celestial track, to drift far from the sun while certain necessary restructuring was carried out. *She knows me,* he realized sickly, watching the pale lips curl around words that meant nothing and everything. *She's met me before.* These things happened in the Stasis; the formal etiquette was deliberate padding to break the soul-shaking impact of such collisions with the consequences of your own future. *She must think I'm an idiot—*

The lecture ended in a flurry of bowing and dismissals. Confused, Pierce found himself standing before the Scholar on the roof of the world, beneath the watching moon. She was very beautiful, and he was utterly mortified. "Honorable Scholar, I don't know how to explain, I—"

"Silence." Yarrow touched one index finger to his lips. His nostrils flared at the scent of her, floral and strange. "I told you to see me in my office. Are you coming?"

Pierce gaped at her. "But Honorable Scholar, I—"

"—forgot that, as your tutor, I am authorized to review your Library record." She smiled secretively. "But I didn't need to: You—your future self—told me why you were distracted, many years-subjective ago. There is a long history between us." Her humor dispersed like mist before a hot wind. "Will you come with me now? And not make an unhappening of our life together?"

"But I—" For the first time he noticed she was using the honorific form of "you," in its most intimate and personal case. "What do you mean, *our* life?"

She began to walk toward the steps leading down to the Northern Courtyard. "*Our* life?" He called after her, dawning anger at the way he'd been manipulated lending his voice an edge. "What do you mean, *our* life?"

She glanced back at him, her expression peculiar—almost wistful. "You'll never know if you don't get over your pride, will you?" Then she looked back at the two hundred stone steps that lay before her, inanimate and treacherous, and began to descend the mountainside. Her gait was as steady and dignified as any matron turning her back on young love and false memories.

He watched her recede for almost a minute before his injured dignity gave way, and he ran after her, stumbling recklessly from step to stone, desperate to discover his future.

HACKING HISTORY

Pleasure Empires

THEY WILL WELCOME YOU as a prince among princes, and they will worship you as a god among gods. They will wipe the sweat from your brow and the dust of the road from your feet, and they will offer to you their sons and daughters and the wine of their vineyards. Their world exists only to please the angels of the celestial court, and we have granted you this leave to dwell among our worshippers, with all the rights and honors of a god made flesh.

They will bring wine unto you, and the fruit of the dream poppy. They will clothe you in silk and gold, and lie naked beneath your feet, and abase themselves before your every whim. They are the people of the Pleasure Empires, established from time to time by the decree of the lords of Stasis to serve their loyal servants, and it is their honor and their duty to obey you and demonstrate their love for you in any way that you desire, for all their days and lifetimes upon the Earth. And you will dwell among them in a palace of alabaster, surrounded by gardens of delight, and you shall want for nothing.

Your days of pleasure will number one thousand and one; your lovers will number a thousand or one as you please; your pleasures will be without number; and the number of tomorrow's parties shall be beyond measure. You need not leave until the pleasures of flesh and mind pale, and the novelty of infinite luxury becomes a weight on your soul. Then and only then, you will yearn for the duty which lends meaning to life; energized, you will return to service with serenity and enthusiasm. And your colleagues will turn aside from their tasks and wonder at your eagerness: for though you may have spent a century in the Pleasure Empires, your absence from your duty will have lasted barely a heartbeat. You are a loyal servant of the Stasis: and you may return to paradise whenever it pleases you, because we want you to be happy in your work.

Palimpsest Ambush

ALMOST A HUNDRED KILOYEARS had passed since the Yellowstone eruption that wiped out the Benzin and the hunter-gatherer tribes of the Gulf Coast. The new

----

Reseeding was twelve thousand years old; civilization had taken root again, spreading around the planet with the efflorescent enthusiasm of a parasitic vine. It was currently going through an expansionist-mercantilist phase, scattered city-states and tribute empires gradually coalescing and moving toward a tentative enlightenment. Eventually they'd rediscover electronics and, with the institution of a ubiquitous surveillance program, finally reconquer the heights of true civilization. Nobody looking at the flourishing cities and the white-sailed trade ships could imagine that the people who built them were destined for anything but glory.

Pierce stumbled along a twisty cobbled lane off the Chandler's Street in Carnegra, doing his faux-drunken best to look like part of the scenery. Sailors fresh ashore from Ipsolian League boats weren't a rarity here, and it'd certainly explain his lack of fluency in Imagra, the local creole. It was another training assignment, but with six more years-subjective of training and a Stasis phone implant, Pierce now had some degree of independence. He was trusted to work away from the watchful eyes of his supervisor, on assignments deemed safe for a probationer-agent.

"Proceed to the Red Duck on Margrave Way at the third hour of Korsday. Take your detox first, and stay on the small beer. You're there as a level-one observer and level-zero exit decoy to cover our other agent's departure. There's going to be a fight, and you need to be ready to look after yourself; but remember, you're meant to be a drunken sailor, so you need to look the

----

part until things kick off. Once your target is out of the picture, you're free to leave. If it turns hot, escalate it to me, and I'll untangle things retroactively."

It was all straightforward stuff, although normally Pierce wouldn't be assigned to a job in Carnegra, or indeed to any job in this epoch. Training to blend in seamlessly with an alien culture was difficult enough that Stasis agents usually worked in their home era, or as close to it as possible, where their local knowledge was most useful. As it was, two months of full-time study had given him just enough background to masquerade as a foreign sailor—in an archipelagean society that was still three centuries away from reinventing the telegraph. *It's a personalized test,* he'd realized with a jittery shudder of alertness, as if he'd just downed a mug of maté. Someone up the line in Operational Analysis would be watching his performance, judging his flexibility. He determined to give it his all.

It took him two months of hard training, in language and cultural studies and local field procedures— all for less than six hours on the ground in Carnegra. And the reason he was certain it was a test: Supervisor Hark had changed the subject when he'd asked who he was there to cover for.

Margrave Way was a cobblestoned alley, stepped every few meters to allow for the slope of the hillside, lined on either side with the single-story bamboo shopfronts of fishmongers and chandlers. Pierce threaded his wobbly way around servants out shopping for the daily catch, water carriers, fruit and vegetable sellers, and beggars; dodged a rice merchant's train of dwarf dromedaries loaded with sacks; and avoided a pair of black-robed scholars from one of the seminaries that straggled around the flanks of the hill like the thinning hair on the pate of an elderly priest. Banners rippled in the weak onshore breeze; paper skull-lanterns with mirror-polished eyes to repel evil spirits bounced gaudily beneath the eaves as he entered the inn.

The Red Duck was painted the color of its namesake. Pierce hunched beneath the low awning and probed the gloom carefully, finally emerging into the yard out back with his eyes watering. At this hour the yard was half-empty, for the tavern made much of its trade in food. The scent of honeysuckle hung heavy over the decking; the hibiscus bushes at the sides of the yard were riotously red. Pierce staked out a bench near the rear wall with a clear view of the entrance and the latrines, then unobtrusively audited the other patrons, careful to avoid eye contact. Even half-empty, the yard held the publican's young sons (shuffling hither and yon to fill cups for the customers), four presumably genuine drunken sailors, three liveried servants from the seminaries, a couple of gaudily clad women whose burlesque approach to the sailors was blatantly professional, and three cloak-shrouded pilgrims from the highlands of what had once been Cascadia—presumably come to visit the shrines and holy baths of the southern lands. At least, to a first approximation.

One of the lads was at Pierce's elbow, asking something about service and food. "Give beer," Pierce managed haltingly. "Good beer light two coin value." The tap-boy vanished, returned with a stoneware mug full of warm suds that smelled faintly of bananas. "Good, good." Pierce fumbled with his change, pawing over it as if unsure. He passed two clipped and blackened coins to the kid—both threaded with passive RF transceivers, beacons to tell his contact that they were not alone.

As Pierce raised his mug to his lips in unfeigned happy anticipation, his phone buzzed. It was a disturbing sensation, utterly unnatural, and it had taken him much practice to learn not to jump when it happened. He scanned the beer garden, concealing his mouth with his mug as he did so. A murder of crows—seminary students flocking to the watering hole—was raucously establishing its pecking order in the vestibule, one of the sailors had fallen forward across the table while his fellow tried to rouse him, and a working girl in a red wrap was walking toward the back wall, humming tunelessly. *Bingo,* he thought, with a smug flicker of satisfaction.

Pierce twitched a stomach muscle, goosing his phone. The other Stasis agent would feel a shiver and buzz like an angry yellow jacket—and indeed, as he watched, the woman in red glanced round abruptly. Pierce twitched again as her gaze flickered over him: this time involuntarily, in the grip of something akin to déjà vu. *Can't be,* he realized an instant later. *She wouldn't be on a field op like this!*

The woman in red turned and sidestepped toward his bench, subvocalizing. *"You're my cover, yes? Let's get out of here right now—it's going bad."*

Pierce began to stand. "Yarrow?" he asked. The sailor who was trying to rouse his friend started tugging at his shoulder.

"Yes? Look, what's your exit plan?" She sounded edgy.

"But—" He froze, his stomach twisting. *She doesn't know me,* he realized. *"Sorry. Can you get over the wall if I create a diversion?"* he sent, his heart hammering. He hadn't seen her in three years-subjective—she'd blown through his life like a runaway train, then vanished as abruptly as she'd arrived, leaving behind a scrawled note to say she'd been called uptime by Control, and a final quick charcoal sketch.

"I think so, but there are two—" The sailor stood up and shouted incoherently at her just as Pierce's phone buzzed again. *"Who's that?"* she asked.

"Hard contact in five seconds!" The other agent, whoever he was, sounded urgent. *"Stay back."*

The sailor shouted again, and this time Pierce understood it: "Murderer!" He climbed over the table and drew a long, curved knife, moving forward.

"Get behind me." Pierce stepped between Yarrow and the sailor, his thoughts a chaotic mess of *This is stupid* and *What did she do?* and *Who else?* as he paged Supervisor Hark. "Peace," he said in faltering Carnegran, "am friend? Want drink?"

Behind the angry sailor the priest-students were standing up, black robes flapping as they spread out, calling to one another. Yarrow retreated behind him: his phone vibrated again, then, improbably, a fourth time. There were too many agents. *"What's happening?"* asked Hark.

"I think it's a palimpsest," Pierce managed to send. Like an inked parchment scrubbed clean and reused, a section of history that had been multiply overwritten. He held his hands up, addressed the sailor, "You want. Thing. Money?"

The third agent, who'd warned of contact: *"Drop. Now!"*

Pierce began to fall as something, someone—*Yarrow?*—grabbed his shoulder and pushed sideways.

One of the students let his robe slide open. It slid down from his shoulders, gaping to reveal an iridescent fluidity that followed the rough contours of a human body, flexing and rippling like molten glass. Its upper margin flowed and swelled around its wearer's neck and chin, bulging upward to engulf his head as he stepped out of the black scholar's robe.

The sailor held his knife high, point down as he advanced on Pierce. Pierce's focus narrowed as he brought his fall under control, preparing to roll and trigger the telescopic baton in his sleeve—

A gunshot, shockingly loud, split the afternoon air. The sailor's head disappeared in a crimson haze, splattering across Pierce's face. The corpse lurched and collapsed like a dropped sack. Somebody—*Yarrow?*—cried out behind him, as Pierce pushed back with his left arm, trying to blink the red fog from his vision.

The student's robe was taking on a life of its own, contracting and standing up like a malign shadow behind its master as the human-shaped blob of walking water turned and raised one hand toward the roof. A chorus of screams rose behind it as one of the other seminarians, who had unwisely reached for the robe, collapsed convulsing.

"Stay down!" It was the third agent. *"Play dead."*

"My knee's—"

Pierce managed a sidelong look that took in Yarrow's expression of fear with a shudder of self-recognition. *"I'll decoy,"* he sent. Then, a curious clarity of purpose in his mind, he rolled sideways and scrambled toward the interior of the tavern.

Several things happened in the next three seconds:

First, a brilliant turquoise circle two meters in diameter flickered open, hovering directly in front of the rear wall of the beer garden. A double handful of enormous purple hornets burst from its surface. Most arrowed toward the students, who had entangled themselves in a panicky crush at the exit: two turned and darted straight up toward the balcony level.

Next, a spark, bright as lightning, leapt between the watery humanoid's upraised hand and the ceiling.

Finally, something punched Pierce in the chest with such breathtaking violence that he found, to his shock and surprise, that his hands and feet didn't seem to want to work anymore.

"Agent down," someone signaled, and it seemed to him that this was something he ought to make sense of, but sense was ebbing fast in a buzz of angry hornets as the pinkness faded to gray. And then everything was quiet for a long time.

Internal Affairs

"Do you know anyone who wants you dead, Scholar-Agent?" The investigator from Internal Affairs leaned over Pierce, his hands clasped together in a manner that reminded Pierce of a hungry mantis. His ears (Pierce couldn't help but notice) were prominent and pink, little radar dishes adorning the sides of a thin face. It had to be an ironic comment if not an outright insult, his adoption of the likeness of Franz Kafka. Or perhaps the man from Internal Affairs simply didn't want to be recognized.

Pierce chuckled weakly. The results were predictable: when the coughing fit subsided, and his vision began to clear again, he shook his head.

"A pity." Kafka rocked backward slightly, his shoulders hunched. "It would make things easier."

Pierce risked a question. "Does the Library have anything?"

Kafka sniffed. "Of course not. Whoever set the trap knew enough to scrub the palimpsest clean before they embarked on their killing spree."

So it was *a palimpsest.* Pierce felt vaguely cheated. "They assassinated themselves first? To remove the evidence from the time sequence?"

"You died three times, Scholar-Agent, not counting your present state." He gestured at the dressing covering the cardiac assist leech clamped to the side of Pierce's chest. It pulsed rhythmically, taking the load while the new heart grew to full size between his ribs. "Agent Yarrow died twice and Agent-Major Alizaid's report states that he was forced to invoke Control Majeure to contain the palimpsest's expansion. *Someone*"—Kafka leaned toward Pierce again, peering intently at his face with disturbingly dark eyes—"went to great lengths to kill you repeatedly."

"Uh." Pierce stared at the ceiling of his hospital room, where plaster cherubs clutching overflowing cornucopiae cavorted with lecherous satyrs. "I suppose you want to know why?"

"No. Having read your Branch Library file, there are any number of *whys*: what I want to know is why *now*." Kafka smiled, his mouth widening until his alarmingly unhinged head seemed ready to topple from the plinth of his jaw. "You're still in training, a green shoot. An interesting time to pick on you, don't you think?"

Fear made Pierce tense up. "If you've read my Library record, you must know I'm loyal…"

"Peace." Kafka made a placating gesture. "I know nothing of the kind; the Library can't tell me what's inside your head. But you're not under suspicion of

----

trying to assassinate yourself. What I *do* know is that so far your career has been notably mundane. The Library branches are as prone to overwrites as any other palimpsest; but we may be able to make deductions about your attacker by looking for inconsistencies between your memories and the version of your history documented locally."

Pierce lay back, drained. *I'm not under suspicion.* "What is to become of me?" he asked.

Kafka's smile vanished. "Nothing, for now: you may convalesce at your leisure, and sooner or later you will learn whatever it is that was so important to our enemies that they tried to erase you. When you do so, I would be grateful if you would call me." He rose to leave. "You will see me again, eventually. Meanwhile, you should bear in mind that you have come to the attention of important persons. Consider yourself lucky—and try to make the best of it."

Three days after Kafka's departure—summoned back, no doubt, to the vasty abyss of deep time in which Internal Affairs held their counsel—Pierce had another visitor.

"I came to thank you," she said haltingly. "You didn't need to do that. To decoy, I mean. I'm very grateful."

It had the sound of a prepared speech, but Pierce didn't mind. She was young and eye-wrenchingly desirable, even in the severe uniform of an Agent Initiate. "You would have died again," he pointed out. "I was your backup. It's bad form to let your primary die. And I owed you."

"You owed me? But we haven't met! There's nothing about you in my Library file." Her pupils dilated.

"It was an older you," he said mildly. While the Stasis held a file on everyone, agents were only permitted to see—and annotate—those of their own details that lay in their past. After a pause, he admitted, "I was hoping we might meet again sometime."

"But I—" She hesitated, then stared at him, narrowing her eyes. "I'm not in the market. I have a partner."

"Funny, she didn't tell me that." He closed his eyes for a few seconds. "She said we had a history, though. And to tell her when I first met her that her first pet—a cat named Chloe—died when a wild dog took her." Pierce opened his eyes to stare at the baroque ceiling again. "I'm sorry I asked, Ya—esteemed colleague. Please forgive me; I didn't think you were for sale. My heart is simply in the wrong place."

After a second he heard a shocked, incongruous giggle.

"I gather armor-piercing rounds usually have that effect," he added.

When she was able to speak again she shook her head. "I am sincere, Scholar-Agent—Pierce?—Pierced? Oh dear!" She managed to hold her dignity intact, this time, despite a gleam of amusement. "I'm sorry if I—I don't mean to doubt you. But you must know, if you know me, *I* have never met *you*, yes?"

"That thought has indeed occurred to me." The leech pulsed warmly against his chest, squirting blood through the aortic shunt. "As you can see, right now I am not only heartless but harmless, insofar as I won't even be able to get out of bed unaided for another ten days; you need not fear that I'm going to pursue you. I merely thought to introduce myself and let you know—as she did to me—that we *could* have a history, if you're so inclined, someday. But not right now. Obviously."

"But obviously not—" She stood up. "This wasn't what I was expecting."

"Me neither." He smiled bitterly. "It never is, is it?"

She paused in the doorway. "I'm not saying no, never, Scholar-Agent. But not now, obviously. Some other time… We'll worry about that if we meet again, perhaps. History can wait a little longer. Oh, and thank you for saving my life some of the times! One out of three is good going, especially for a student."

ELITE

A Brief Alternate History of the Solar System: Part One

What has already happened:

Slide 1.

Our solar system, as an embryo. A vast disk of gas and infalling dust surrounds and obscures a newborn star, little more than a thickening knot of rapidly spinning matter that is rapidly sucking more mass down into its ever-steepening gravity well. The sun is glowing red-hot already with the heat liberated by its gravitational collapse, until...

SLIDE 2.

Ignition! The pressure and temperature at the core of the embryo star has risen so high that hydrogen nuclei floating in a degenerate soup of electrons are bumping close to one another. A complex reaction ensues, rapidly liberating gamma radiation and neutrinos, and the core begins to heat up. First deuterium, then the ordinary hydrogen nuclei begin to fuse. A flare of nuclear fire lashes through the inner layers of the star. It will take a million years for the gamma-ray pulse to work its way out through the choking, blanketing layers of degenerate hydrogen, but the neutrino pulse heralds the birth cry of a new star.

SLIDE 3.

A million years pass as the sun brightens, and the rotating cloud of gas and dust begins to partition. Out beyond the dew line, where ice particles can grow, a roiling knot of dirty ice is forming, and like the sun before it, it greedily sucks down dirt and gas and grows. As it plows through the cloud, it sprays dust outward. Meanwhile, at the balancing point between the star and the embryonic Jovian gravity well, other knots of dust are forming...

SLIDE 4.

A billion years have passed since the sun ignited, and the stellar nursery of gas and dust has been swept clean by a fleet of new-formed planets. There has been some bickering—in the late heavy bombardment triggered by the outward migration of Neptune, entire planetary surfaces were re-formed— but now the system has settled into long-term stability. The desert planet Mars is going through the first of its warm, wet interludes; Venus still has traces of water in its hot (but not yet red-hot) atmosphere. Earth is a chilly nitrogen-and-methane-shrouded enigma inhabited only by primitive purple bacteria, its vast oceans churned by hundred-meter tides dragged up every seven-hour day by a young moon that completes each orbit in little more than twenty-four hours.

SLIDE 5.

Another three billion years have passed. The solar system has completed almost sixteen orbits of the galactic core, and is now unimaginably distant from the stellar nursery which birthed it. Mars has dried, although occasional volcanic eruptions periodically blanket it in cloud. Venus is even hotter. But something strange is happening to Earth. Luna has drifted farther from its primary, the tides quieting; mean-while, the atmosphere has acquired a strange bluish tinge, evident sign of contamination by a toxic haze of oxygen. The great landmass Rodina, which dom-inated the southern ocean beneath a cap of ice, has broken up and the shallow seas of the Panthalassic and Panafrican Oceans are hosting an astonishing proliferation of multicellular life.

SLIDE 6.

Six hundred and fifty million years later, the outlines of Earth's new continents glow by night like a neon diadem against the darkness, shouting consciousness at the sky in a blare of radio-wavelength emissions as loud as a star.

There have been five major epochs dominated by different families of land-based vertebrates in the time between slides 5 and 6. All the Earth's coal and oil deposits were laid down in this time, different animal families developed flight at least four times, and the partial pressure of oxygen in the atmosphere rose from around 4 percent to well over 16 percent. At the very end, a strangely bipedal, tailless omnivore appeared on the plains of Africa—its brain turbocharged on a potent mixture of oxygen and readily available sugars—and erupted into sentience in a geological eyeblink.

HERE'S WHAT ISN'T GOING TO HAPPEN:

SLIDE 7.

The continents of Earth, no longer lit by the afterglow of intelligence, will drift into strange new configurations. Two hundred and fifty million years after the sixth great extinction, the scattered continents will reconverge on a single equatorial supercontinent, Pangea Ultima, leaving only the conjoined landmass that was Antarctica and Australia adrift in the southern ocean. As the sun brightens, so shall the verdant plains of the Earth; oceanic algal blooms raise the atmospheric oxygen concentration close to 25 percent, and lightning-triggered wildfires rage across the continental interior. It will be an epoch characterized by rapid plant growth, but few animal life-forms can survive on land—in the heady air of aged Earth, even waterlogged flesh will burn. And the sun is still brightening...

SLIDE 8.

Seven hundred and fifty million years later. The brightening sun will glare down upon cloud-wreathed ancient continents, weathered and corroded to bedrock. Even the plant life has abandoned the land, for the equatorial daytime temperature is perilously close to the boiling point of water. What life there is retreats to the deep ocean waters, away from the searing ultraviolet light that splits apart the water molecules of the upper atmosphere. But there's no escape: the oceans themselves are slowly acidifying and evaporating as the hydrogen liberated in the ionosphere is blasted into space by the solar wind. A runaway greenhouse effect is well under way, and in another billion years Earth will resemble parched, hell-hot Venus.

SLIDE 9.

Four-point-two billion years after the brief cosmic eyeblink of Earthly intelligence, the game is up. The dead Earth orbits alone, its moon a separate planet wandering in increasingly unstable ellipses around the sun. Glowing dull red beneath an atmosphere of carbon dioxide baked from its rocks, there will be no sign that this world ever harbored life. The sun it circles, a sullen-faced ruddy ogre, is nearing the end of its hydrogen reserves. Soon it will expand, engulfing the inner planets.

But events on a larger scale are going to spare the Earth this fate. For billions of years, the galaxy in which this star orbits has been converging with another large starswarm, the M-31 Andromeda galaxy. Now the spiraling clouds of stars are interpenetrating and falling through each other, and the sun is in for a bumpy ride as galaxies collide.

A binary system of red dwarfs is closing with the solar system at almost five hundred kilometers per second. They are going to pass within half a billion kilometers of the sun, a hairbreadth miss in cosmic terms: in the process they will wreak havoc on the tidy layout of the solar system. Jupiter, dragged a few million kilometers sunward, will enter an unstable elliptical orbit, and over the course of a few thousand years it will destabilize all the other planets. Luna departs first, catapulted out of the plane of the ecliptic; Earth, most massive of all, will spend almost five million years wobbling between the former orbits of Venus and Saturn before it finally caroms past Jupiter and drifts off into the eternal night, the tattered remnants of its atmosphere condensing and freezing in a shroud of dry ice.

Slow Recovery

PIERCE WAS TO REMAIN on official convalescent leave for an entire year-subjective. His heart had been torn to shreds by a penetrator round; repairing the peripheral damage, growing a new organ in situ, and restoring him to physical condition was a nontrivial matter. Luckily for him, the fatal shooting had happened in the middle of a multiple-overwrite ambush that was finally shut down by Control Majeure using weapons of gross anachronism, and they'd whisked his bleeding wreckage out through a timegate before he'd finished drumming his heels.

Nevertheless, organ regeneration—not to mention psychological recovery from a violent fatal injury— took time. So, rather than shipping him straight to the infirmary in the alpine monastery in Training Zone 25, he was sent to recover in the Rebirth Wing of the Chrysanthemum Clinic, on the Avenue of the Immortals of Medicine, in the city of Leng, on the northeastern seaboard of the continent of Nova Zealantis, more than four billion years after the time into which he had been born.

The current Reseeding was Enlightened; not only were they aware of the existence of the Stasis, but they were a part of the greater transtemporal macroculture: speakers of Urem, obedient to the Stasis, even granted dispensation to petition for use of the timegate in extraordinary circumstances. In return, the Hegemony was altogether conscientious in observing their duties to the guardians of history, according Pierce honors that, in other ages, might have been accorded to a diplomat or minor scion of royalty. Unfortunately, this entailed rather more formality than Pierce was used to. The decor, for one thing: they'd clearly studied his epoch, but modeling his hospital suite on Louis XV's bedroom at Versailles suggested they had strange ideas about his status.

"If it pleases you, my lord, would you like to describe how you entered the celestial service?" The journalist, who his bowing and shuffling concierge explained had been sent by the city archive to document his life, was young, pretty, and shiny-eyed. She'd obviously studied his public records and the customs of his home civilization, and decided to go for the throat. Local fashion echoed the Minoan empire of antiquity, and her attire, though scholarly, was disconcerting: a flash of well-turned ankle, nipples rouged and ringed—Pierce realized he was staring and turned his face away, chagrined.

"Please?" she repeated, her plump lower lip quivering. Her cameras flittered below the ceiling like lazy bluebottles, iridescent in the afternoon sunlight, logging her life for posterity.

"I suppose so..." Pierce trailed off, staring through the open window at the lower slopes of the hillside on which the clinic nestled. "But there's no secret, really, none at all. You don't approach them—they approach you. A tap on the shoulder at the right time, an offer of a job, at first I didn't think it was anything unusual."

"Was there anything leading up to that? My lord? What was your life like before the service?"

Pierce frowned slightly as he forced his sullen memory to work. There were gaps. "I'm not sure; I think I was in a car crash, or maybe a war..."

His cardiac leech pulsed against his chest like a contented cat. Sunlight warmed the side of his face as he watched her sidelong, from the corner of his eye. *How far will she go for a story?* he wondered idly. *Play your cards right and...well, maybe.* His temporarily heartless condition had rendered amorous speculations—or anything else calculated to raise the blood pressure—purely academic for the time being.

"My lord?" He pretended to miss the moue of annoyance that flitted across her face, but the very deliberate indrawn breath that followed it was so transparent that he nearly gave the game away by laughing.

"I'm not your lord," he said gently. "I'm just a scholar-agent, halfway through my twenty years of training. What I know about the Guardians of Time"—that was what the Hegemonites called the Stasis, those in power who had polite words for them—"and can tell you is mere trivia. I'm sure your Archive already has it all."

This was a formally declared Science Epoch, in which a whole series of consecutive Reseedings were dedicated to collating the mountain-sized chunks of data returned by the Von Neumann probes that had been launched during the last Science Epoch, a billion years earlier. They and their descendants had quietly fanned out throughout the local group of galaxies, traveling at barely a hundredth of the speed of light, visiting and mapping every star system and extrasolar planet within ten million light-years. There was a lot of material to collate; The Zealantian Hegemony's army of elite astrocartographers, millions strong, would labor for tens of thousands of years to assemble just their one corner of the big picture. And their obsession with knowledge didn't stop at the edge of the solar system.

("A civilization of obsessive-compulsive stamp collectors," Wei had called them when he briefly visited his ex-student. "You've got to watch these Science Cults; sooner or later they'll turn all the carbon in the deep biosphere into memory diamond, then where will we be?")

"The Archive doesn't know everything, my lord. It's not like the Library of Time." There was a strangely reverent note in her voice, as if the Library was somehow different. "We don't have permission to read the forbidden diaries, my lord. We have to accept whatever crusts of wisdom our honored guests choose to let fall from their trenchers."

"I'm not your lord. You can call me Pierce, if you like."

"Yes, my, ah. Pierce? My lord."

"What should I call you?" he asked after a pause.

"Me? I am nobody, Lord Pierce! I am a humble journal-keeper—"

"Rubbish." He looked directly at her, taking in everything: her flounced scholar-lady's dress, the jeweled rings through her ears and nipples, her painstakingly knotted chignon. This was a high-energy civilization, but a very staid, conservative one with strict sumptuary laws: were she a commoner, she would risk a flogging for indecency, or worse, dressing above her station. "Who are you really? And why are you so interested in *me*?"

"Oh! If you *must* know, I am doctor-postulant Xiri, daughter of doctor doctor professor archivist His Excellency Dean Imad of the College of History, and Her Ladyship doctor professor emeritus Leila of the faculty of hot super-Jovian moons"—she smiled coyly—"and I have been charged, by my duty and my honor as a scholar, to study you in absolute detail by my tutors. They have assigned you to me as the topic of my first dissertation. On the hero-guardians of time."

"Your *first* dissertation—" Her parents were a professor and a dean; she might as well have said *sheikh* or *baron*. "Do I have any choice in the matter?"

"You can refuse, of course." She shivered and tugged her filmy shawl back into position. "But *I* can't."

"Why? What happens if you refuse?"

She shivered. "I would forfeit my doctorate. The shame! My parents"—for a moment the bright-eyed optimism cracked—"would blame themselves. It would cast doubt on my commitment."

Was failure to make tenure track justification for an honor killing? Pierce shook his head, staring at her. "I'm just a trainee!" He reached for the bed's control, stabbing the button to raise his back. The interview was out of control, heading for deep waters, and lying down gave him an unaccountable fear of drowning. "*I'm* the nobody around here!"

"How do you know that, my lord? For all you know, you might be destined for glory." She tugged at her shawl again and smiled, an ingenue trying to look mysterious.

"But I don't have any—" He switched off the bed lift once he was level with her, looked her in the eyes, and changed the subject in midsentence. "Have your people ever met me before?"

The hardest part of arguing with her, he found, was avoiding staring at her chest. She was really very pretty, but her pedigree suggested he'd be wise to abandon that line of thought; she'd be about as safe to seduce as a rattlesnake.

"No." Her smile widened. "A handsome man of mystery and a time hero to boot: yes, they told us why you were here." Her gaze briefly covered his chest.

For the first time in many months, Pierce resorted to his native language. "Oh, *hell*." He glanced at the window, then back at Xiri. "Everybody wants to study me," he confessed. "I don't know why, I really don't…" He crossed his arms, looked at her. "Study away. I am at your disposal." At least it promised to be a less harrowing experience than Kafka's cross-examination.

"Oh! Thank you, my lord!" She placed a proprietorial hand on the side of his bed. "I will do my utmost to make it an enjoyable experience."

"Really?" There was something about her tone of voice that took him aback, as if he'd answered a question that he didn't remember being asked. The idea of being studied struck Pierce as marginally more enjoyable than banging his head on the wall, but on the upside, Xiri was high-quality eye candy. On the downside—*Don't go there,* he reminded himself. "Where would you like to begin?"

"Right here, I think," she said, sliding her hand under the covers.

"Hey! I! Huh." Pierce found, to his mild alarm, that her busy hand was getting results. "Um. I don't want to sound ungrateful, but we really shouldn't—why are you—aren't you going to shut off your cameras—"

"I have read about your culture." She sat down on the bed beside him with a rustle of silk. "In some ways, it sounded very familiar. Did they not record everything that happened to them? Did they not talk about people marrying their work? Well, that is just how we do that here."

"But that's just a metaphor!" He tried to push her hand away, but his heart wasn't in it.

"Hush." She responded by making him shudder. "You're the subject of my dissertation! I'm going to find out *all* about you. It's to be my life's work! I'm so

----

happy! Just relax, my lord, and everything will be wonderful. Don't worry, I have studied the customs of your time, and they are not so very alien. We can talk about the wedding tomorrow, after you've met my father."

EMPTY MANSIONS

RESISTANCE WAS FUTILE: NEARLY twenty years-subjective passed Pierce by with the eyeblink impact of another bullet, half of them shared with his new wife. Xiri, true to her word, wrapped her life around his twisted time line: at first as an adoring wife, and then, to his bemused and growing pride, mother to three small children and doctor-professor in her own right. Her dissertation was his life: merely glancing lightly off the skin of time was, it seemed, a passport to wealth and status in the Hegemony, and he found life as the consort of a beautiful noblewoman no less congenial than he might have expected.

Xiri did not complain at Pierce's eyeblink excursions from their family home (provided by the grace of her father the dean), which usually lasted only for seconds of subjective time. Nor did she complain about the inward-looking silences and moody introspection that followed, and were of altogether greater duration. On the contrary: they invariably provided additional data for her life's work, once she delicately untangled the story from his memories of unhistory. Sometimes he would age an entire year in an hour's working absence, but the medical privileges of the Stasis extended also to the Enlightened; there would be plenty of time to catch up, over the decades and centuries.

Pierce, for his part, found it oddly easier to deal with the second half of his training with a stable family life to fall back on. The Stasis were spread surprisingly thin across their multitrillion-year empire. The defining characteristic of his job seemed to be that he was only called for in turbulent, interesting times. Between peak oil and Spanish flu, from Carthage to the Cold War, his three-thousand-year beat sometimes seemed no more than a vale of tears—and a thin, poor, nightmare of a world at that, far from the mannered, drowsy contentment of the ten-thousand-year-long Hegemony. Most of his fellow students seemed to prefer the hedonistic abandon proffered by the Pleasure Empires, but Pierce held his own counsel and congratulated himself on his discovery of a more profound source of satisfaction.

On his first return to training after his convalescence, Pierce was surprised to be summoned to Superintendent-of-Scholars Manson's chambers.

"You have formed attachments while convalescing." Manson fixed him with a watery stare. "That is inadvisable, as you will no doubt learn for yourself. However, Operations have noted that there is no permanent Resident in place within a millennium either side of your, ah, domestic anchor-point. It is a tranquil society, but not *that* tranquil; you are therefore instructed and permitted to maintain your attachment and develop your ability to work there. Purely as a secondary specialty, you understand."

Pierce had almost fallen over with shock. Once he regained his self-control, he asked, "To whom shall I report, master?"

"To your wife, student. Tell her to write up everything. We read all such dissertations, in the end."

Manson looked away, dismissing him. Pierce nudged his phone, weak-kneed, not trusting his ability to make a dignified exit; after a brief routing delay, the timegate responded to his heartfelt wish, and the ground opened up and swallowed him.

One day very late in his training, with perhaps half a year-subjective remaining until his graduation as a full-fledged agent of the Stasis, Pierce returned home from a week sampling the plague-pits of fourteenth-century Constantinople. He found Xiri in an unusually excited state, the household all abuzz around her. "It's fantastic!" she exclaimed, hurrying to meet him across the atrium of their summer residence. "Did you know about it? Tell me you knew about it! *This* was why you came to our time, wasn't it?"

Pierce, greeting her with a fond smile, lifted young Magnus (who had been attempting to scale his back, with much snarling, presumably to slay the giant) and handed him to his nursemaid. "What's happened?" he asked mildly, trying to give no sign of the frisson he'd momentarily felt (for their youngest son could have no idea of how his father had just spent a week taking tissue samples, carving chunks of mortal flesh from the bubo-stricken bodies of boys of an age to be his playmates in another era). "What's got everyone so excited?"

"It's the probes! They've found something outra-geous in Messier 33, six thousand light-years along the third arm!"

Pierce—who could not imagine finding anything outrageous in a galaxy over a million light-years away, even if mapping it *was* the holy raison d'être of this Civilization—decided to humor his wife. "Indeed. And tell me, what precisely is there that brings forth such outrage? As opposed to mere excitement, or curiosity, or perplexity?"

"Look!" Xiri gestured at the wall, which oblig-ingly displayed a dizzying black void sprinkled with stars. "Let's see. Wall, show me the anomaly I was discussing with the honorable doctor-professor Zun about two hours ago. Set magnification level plus forty, pan left and up five—there! You see it!"

Pierce stared for a while. "Looks like just another rock to me," he said. Racking his brains for the correct form: "an honorable sub-Earth, airless, of the third degree, predominantly siliceous. Yes?"

"Oh!" Xiri, nobly raised, did nothing so undigni-fied as to stamp her foot; nevertheless, Magnus's nurse-maid swept up her four-year-old charge and beat a hasty retreat. (Xiri, when excited, could be as dangerously prone to eruption as a Wolf-Rayet star.) "Is that all you can see? Wall, magnification plus ten, repeat step, step, step. *There.* Look at that, my lord, look!"

The airless moon no longer filled the center of the wall; now it stretched across it from side to side, so close that there was barely any visible curvature to its horizon. Pierce squinted. Craters, rills, drab, irregular features and a scattering of straight-edged rectangular crystals. *Crystals?* He chewed on the thought, found it curiously lacking as an explanation for the agitation. Gradually, he began to feel a quiet echo of his wife's excitement. "What are they?"

"They're buildings! Or they were, sixty-six million years ago, when the probes were passing through. And we didn't put them there…"

THE LIBRARY AT THE END OF TIME

A Brief Alternate History of the Solar System: Part Two

. . . And then the Stasis happened:

Slide 7.

After two hundred and fifty million years, the continents of Earth, strobe-lit by the mayfly flicker of empires, will have converged on a single equatorial supercontinent, Pangea Ultima. These will not be good times for humanity; the vast interior deserts are arid and the coastlines subject to vast hurricanes sweeping in from the world-ocean. As the sun brightens, so shall the verdant plains of the

Earth; but the Stasis have long-laid plans to deflect the inevitable.

Deep in the asteroid belt, their swarming robot cockroaches have dismantled Ceres, used its mass to build a myriad of solar-sail-powered flyers. Now a river of steerable rocks with the mass of a dwarf planet loops down through the inner system, converting solar energy into momentum and transferring it to the Earth through millions of repeated flybys.

Already, Earth has migrated outward from the sun. Other adjustments are under way, subtle and far-reaching: the entire solar system is slowly changing shape, creaking and groaning, drifting toward a new and more useful configuration. Soon—in cosmological terms—it will be unrecognizable.

SLIDE 8.

A billion years later, the Earth lies frozen and fallow, its atmosphere packed down to snow and nitrogen vapor in the chilly wilderness beyond Neptune. *This* was never part of the natural destiny of the homeworld, but it is only a temporary state—for in another ten million years, the endlessly cycling momentum shuttles will crank Earth closer to the sun. Fifty million years after that, the Reseedings will recommence, from the prokaryotes and algae on up; but in this era, the Stasis want the Earth safely mothballed while their technicians from the Engineering Republics work their magic.

For thirty million years the Stasis will devote their timegate to lifting mass from the heart of a burning star, channeling vast streams of blazing plasma into massive, gravitationally bound bunkers, reserves against a chilly future. The sun will gutter and fade to red, raging and flaring in angry outbursts as its internal convection systems collapse. As it shrinks and dims, they will inflict the final murderous insult, and inject an embryonic black hole into the stellar core. Eating mass faster than it can reradiate it through Hawking radiation, the hole will grow, gutting the stellar core.

By the time the Earth drops back toward the frost line of the solar system, the technicians will have roused the zombie necrosun from its grave. Its accretion disk—fed with mass steadily siphoned from the brown dwarfs orbiting on the edges of the system—will cast a strange, harsh glare across Earth's melting ice caps.

Replacing the fusion core of the sun with a mass-crushing singularity is one of the most important tasks facing the Stasis; annihilation is orders of magnitude more efficient than fusion, not to say more controllable, and the mass they have so carefully husbanded is sufficient to keep the closely orbiting Earth lit and warm not for billions, but for trillions of years to come.

But another, more difficult task remains...

SLIDE 9.

Four and a quarter billion years after the awakening of consciousness, and the Milky Way and Andromeda galaxies will collide. The view from Earth's crowded continents is magnificent, like a chaos of burning diamond dust strewn across the emptiness void. Shock waves thunder through the gas clouds, creating new stellar nurseries, igniting millions of massive, short-lived new stars; for a brief ten-million-year period, the nighttime sky will be lit by a monthly supernova fireworks display. The huge black holes at the heart of each galaxy have shed their robes of dust and gas and blaze naked in ghastly majesty as they streak past each other, ripping clusters of stars asunder and seeding more, in a starburst of cosmic fireworks that will be visible nearly halfway across the universe.

But Earth is safe. Earth is serene. Earth is no longer in the firing line.

The Long Burn is by far the largest program of the Stasis. Science Empires will rise and flourish, decay and gutter into extinction, to provide the numerical feedstock for the Navigators. The delicate task of ejecting a star system from its galaxy without setting the planets and moons adrift in their orbits is monstrously difficult. Planets are not bound to their stars by physical cords, and gravity is weak; innumerable adjustments to the orbits of all the significant planets will be required if they are to be carried along. The mass flow of Ceres alone will not suffice. Rocky Mercury has already been dismantled to provide the control mechanisms that keep the necrostar's accretion disk burning steadily; it's Venus's turn to supply the swarming light-sail-driven mass tugs. A brown dwarf ten times the size of Jupiter will fuel the rocket, an entire stellar embryo pumped down to the blazing maw in the course of a million years.

Galactic escape velocity is high, and escape velocity from the local group is even higher. The Long Burn will last ten thousand centuries. Each year that passes, the necrostar will be moving a meter per second faster. And when it comes to an end, the drastically redesigned solar system will be racing away from the local group of galaxies at almost a thousandth the speed of light—straight toward the Bootes Void.

SLIDE 10.

Over the next billion years, Starship Earth and its dead star will rendezvous with the other components of their lifeboat fleet; an even hundred brown dwarf stars, ten to fifty times as massive as Jupiter and every last one dislodged and sent tumbling from its home galaxy by the robot probes of the Engineering Empires.

Their mass will be gratefully received. For Earth is going on a voyage of discovery, where no star has gone before, into the heart of darkness.

CONTINENT OF LIES

NOTHING IN HIS EARLIER life had prepared Pierce for what came next. It beggared belief: a series of synthetic aperture radar scans transmitted by a probe millions of years ago in another galaxy had triggered a diplomatic crisis, threatening world war and civilizational autocide.

The Hegemony, despite being a Science Empire, was not the only nation in this age. (True world governments were rare, cumbersome dinosaurs notorious for their absolute top-down corruption and catastrophic-failure modes: the Stasis tended to discourage them.) The Hegemony shared their world with the Autonomous Directorate of Zan, a harshly abstemious land of puritanical library scientists (located on a continent which had once been attached to North America and Africa); sundry secular monarchies, republics, tyrannies, autarchies, and communes (who thought their superpower neighbors mildly insane for wasting so much of their wealth on academic institutions, rather than the usual aimless and undirected pursuit of human happiness); and the Kingdom of Blattaria (whose inhabitants obeyed the prehistoric prophet Haldane with fanatical zeal, studying the *arthropoda* in ecstatic devotional raptures).

The Hegemony was geographically the largest of the great powers, unified by a set of common filing and monitoring protocols; but it was not a monolithic entity. The authorities of the western principality of Stongu (special area of study: the rocky moons of Hot Jupiters in M-33) had reacted to the discovery of Civilization on the moon of a water giant with a spectacular display of sour grapes, accusing the northeastern Zealantians of *fabricating data* in a desperate attempt to justify a hit-and-run raid on the Hegemony's federal tax base. Quite what the academics of Leng were supposed to do with these funds was never specified, nor was it necessary to say any more in order to get the blood boiling in the seminaries and colleges. *Fabricating data* had a deadly ring to it in any Science Empire, much like the words *crusade* and *jihad* in the millennium prior to Pierce's birth. Once the accusation had been raised, it could not be ignored—and this presented the Hegemony with a major internal problem.

"Honored soldier of the Guardians of Time, our gratitude would be unbounded were you to choose to intercede for us," said the speaker for the delegation from the Dean's Lodge that called on his household barely two days after the discovery. "We would not normally dream of petitioning your eminence, but the geopolitical implications are alarming."

And indeed, they were; for the Hegemony supplied information to the Autonomous Directorate, in return for the boundless supplies of energy harvested by the solar collectors that blanketed the Directorate's inland deserts. Allegations of *fabricating data* could damage the value of the Hegemony's currency; indeed, the aggressive and intolerant Zanfolk might consider it grounds for war (and an excuse for yet another of their tiresome attempts to obtain the vineyards and breadbasket islands of the Outer Nesh archipelago).

"I will do what I can." Pierce bowed deeply to the delegates, who numbered no less than a round dozen deans and even a vice-chancellor or two: he studiously avoided making eye contact with his father-in-law, who stood at the back. "If you are absolutely sure of the merits of your case, I can consult the Library, then testify publicly, insofar as I am authorized to do so. Would that be acceptable?"

The vice-chancellor of the Old College of Leng— an institution with a history of over six thousand years at this point—bowed in return, his face stiff with gratitude. "We are certain of our case, and consequently willing to abide by the word of the Library of the Guardians of Time. Please permit me to express my gratitude once more—"

After half an hour of formalities, the delegation finally departed. Xiri reemerged from her seclusion to direct the servants and robots in setting the receiving room of their mansion aright; the boys also emerged, showing no sign of understanding what had just happened. "Xiri, I need to go to the Final Library," Pierce told her, taking her hands in his and watching for signs of understanding.

"Why, that's wonderful, is it not? My lord? Pierce?" She stared into his eyes. "Why are you worried?"

Pierce swallowed bitter saliva. "The Library is not a place, Xiri; it's a *time*. It contains the sum total of all recorded human knowledge, after the end of humanity. I'm near to graduation, I'm allowed to go there to use it, but it's not—it's not *safe*. Sometimes people who go to the Library disappear and don't come back. And sometimes they come back changed. It's not just a passive archive."

Xiri nodded, but looked skeptical. "But what kind of danger can it pose, given the question you're going to put to it? You're just asking for confirmation that we've been honoring our sources. That's not like asking for the place and time of your own death, is it?"

"I hope you're right, but I don't know for sure." Pierce paused. "That's the problem." He raised her hands to his lips and kissed the backs of her fingers. *If it must be done, best do it fast.* "I'll go and find out. I'll be back soon..."

He stepped back a pace and activated his phone. *"Agent-Trainee Pierce, requesting a Library slot."*

There was a brief pause while the relays stored his message, awaited a transmission slot, then fired them through the timegate to Control. Then he felt the telltale buzzing in the vicinity of his left kidney that warned of an incoming wormhole. It opened around him, spinning out and engulfing him in scant milliseconds, almost too fast to see: then he was no longer standing in the hall of his own mansion but on a dark plain of artificial limestone, facing a doorway set into the edge of a vast geodesic dome made from some translucent material: the Final Library.

A Brief Alternate History of the Solar System: Part Three

SLIDE 11.

ONE HUNDRED BILLION YEARS will pass.

Earth orbits a mere twenty million kilometers from its necrosun in this epoch, and the fires of the accretion disk are banked. Continents jostle and shudder, rising and falling, as the lights strobe around their edges (and occasionally in low equatorial orbit, whenever the Stasis permits a high-energy civilization to arise).

By the end of the first billion years of the voyage, the night skies are dark and starless. The naked eye can still—barely, if it knows where to look—see the Chaos galaxy formed by the collision of M-31 and the Milky Way; but it is a graveyard, its rocky planets mostly supernova-sterilized iceballs ripped from their parent stars by one close encounter too many. Unicellular life (once common in the Milky Way, at least) has taken a knock; multicellular life (much rarer) has received a mortal body blow. Only the Stasis's lifeboat remains.

Luna still floats in Terrestrial orbit—it is a useful tool to stir Earth's liquid core. Prone to a rocky sclerosis, the Earth's heart is a major problem for the Stasis. They can't let it harden, lest the subduction cycle and the deep carbon cycle on which the biosphere depends grind to a halt. But there are ways to stir it up again.

They can afford to wait half a billion years for the Earth to cool, then reseed the reborn planet with archaea and algae. After the first fraught experiment in reterraforming, the Stasis find it sufficient to reboot the mantle and outer core once every ten billion years or so.

The universe changes around them, slowly but surely.

At the end of a hundred billion years, uranium no longer exists in useful quantities in the Earth's crust. Even uranium 238 decays eventually, and twenty one half-lives is more than enough to render it an exotic memory, like the bright and early dawn of the universe. Other isotopes will follow suit, leaving only the most stable behind.

(The Stasis have sufficient for their needs, and might even manufacture more—were it necessary—using the necrostar's ergosphere as a forge. But the Stasis don't particularly want their clients to possess the raw materials for nuclear weapons. Better by far to leave those tools by the wayside.)

The sky is dark. The epoch of star formation has drawn to a close in the galaxies the Earth has left. No bright new stellar nurseries glitter in the void. All the bright, fast-burning suns have exploded and faded. All the smaller main-sequence stars have bloated into dyspeptic ruddy giants, then exhausted their fuel and collapsed. Nothing bright remains save a scattering of dim red and white dwarf stars.

Smaller bodies—planets, moons, and comets—are slowly abandoning their galaxies, shed from stars as their orbits become chaotic, then ejecting at high speed from the galaxy itself in the wake of near encounters with neighboring stars. Like gas molecules in the upper atmosphere of a planet warmed by a star, the lightest leave first. But the process is inexorable. The average number of planets per star is falling slowly.

(About those gas molecules: the Stasis have, after some deliberation, taken remedial action. Water vapor is split by ultraviolet light in the upper atmosphere, and the Earth can ill afford to lose its hydrogen. A soletta now orbits between Earth and the necro-sun, filtering out the short-wavelength radiation, and when they periodically remelt the planet to churn the magma, they are at pains to season their new-made hell with a thousand cometary hydrogen carriers. But eventually more extreme measures will be necessary.)

The sky is quiet and deathly cold. The universe is expanding, and the wavelength of the cosmic microwave background radiation has stretched. The temperature of space itself is now only thousandths of a degree above absolute zero. The ripples in the background are no longer detectable, and the distant quasars have reddened into invisibility. Galactic clusters that were once at the far edge of detection are now beyond the cosmic event horizon, and though Earth has only traveled two hundred million light-years from the Local Group, the gulf behind it is nearly a billion light-years wide. This is no longer a suitable epoch for Science Empires, for the dynamic universe they were called upon to study is slipping out of sight.

SLIDE 12.

A trillion years will pass.

The universe beyond the necrosun's reach is black. Far behind it, the final stars of the Local Group have burned out. White dwarfs have cooled to the temperature of liquid water; red dwarfs have guttered into chilly darkness. Occasionally stellar remnants collide, then the void is illuminated by flashes of lightning, titanic blasts of radiation as the supernovae and gamma-ray bursters flare.

But the explosions are becoming rare. Now it isn't just planets that are migrating away from the chilly corpses of the galaxies. Stellar remnants are ejected into the void as the galaxies themselves fall apart with age.

Space is empty and cold, barely above absolute zero. The necrostar's course has passed through what was once the Bootes Void, but there is no end to the emptiness in sight: there are voids in all directions now. The Stasis and their clients have abandoned the practice of astronomy. They maintain a simple radar watch in the direction of travel, sending out a gigawatt ping every year against the tiny risk of a rogue asteroid, but they haven't encountered an extrasolar body larger than a grain of sand for billions of years.

As for the necrosun's planetary attendants...

One day they will burn Jupiter to keep themselves warm. And Saturn, and icy Neptune, water bunker for the oceans of Earth. These days have not yet come, for they are still working through the titans, through Rhea and Oceanus, Crius and Hyperion— the brown dwarfs built with Sol's stolen mass, and the other dwarfs stolen from the Milky Way during the Long Burn. Each brown dwarf burns for many times the age of the universe at the birth of humanity; black holes are nothing if not efficient. But one day they will be used up, the last titan reduced to a dwarfish cinder; and it will be time to start eating the planets.

Not long thereafter, it will be time for the final Reseeding.

Spin Control

PIERCE STOOD UNCERTAINLY BEFORE the door in the dome. It glowed blue-green with an inner light, and when he looked around, his shadow stretched into the night behind him.

"Don't wait outside for too long," someone said waspishly. *"The air isn't safe."*

The air? Pierce wondered as he entered the doorway. The glassy slabs of an airlock slid aside and closed behind him, thrice in rapid succession. He found himself in a spacious vivarium, illuminated by a myriad of daylight-bright lamps shining from the vertices of the dome wall's triangular segments. There were plants everywhere, green and damp-smelling cycads and ferns and crawling, climbing vines. Insect life hidden in the undergrowth creaked and rattled loudly.

Then he noticed the Librarian, who stood in the clearing before the doors, as unnaturally still as a plastinated corpse.

"I haven't been here before," Pierce admitted as he approached the robed figure. "I've used outlying branches, but never the central Library itself."

"I know." The Librarian pushed back the hood of his robe to reveal a plump, bald head, jowly behind its neat goatee, and gimlet eyes that seemed to drill straight through him.

Pierce stopped, uncertain. "Do I know you?"

"Almost certainly not. Call me Torque. Or Librarian." Torque pointed to a path through the vegetation. "Come, walk with me. I'll show you to your reading room, and you can get started. You might want to bookmark this location in case you need to return."

Pierce nodded. "Is there anybody else here?"

"Not at present." Torque sniffed. "You and I are the only living human beings on the planet right now, although there may be more than one of you present. You have the exclusive use of the Library's resources this decade, within reason."

"Within reason?"

"Sometimes our supervisors—yours or mine— take an interest. They are not required to notify me of their presence." There was a fork in the path, around a large outcropping of some sort of rock crystal, like quartz; Torque turned left. "Ah, here we are. This is your reading room, Student-Agent Pierce."

A white-walled roofless cubicle sat in the middle of a clearing, through which ran a small brook, its banks overgrown with moss and ferns. The walls were only shoulder high, a formality and a signifier of privacy; they surrounded a plain wooden desk and a chair. "This is everything?" Pierce asked, startled.

"Not entirely. Look up." Torque gestured at the dome above them. "In here we maintain a human-compatible biosphere to reprocess your air and waste. We provide light, and heat, although the latter is less important than it will be in a few million years hereabouts. We've turned down the sun to conserve mass, but it's still radiating brightly in the infrared; the real problems will start when we work through the last bunker reserve in about eighteen million years. The dome should keep the Library accessible to readers for about thirty million years after that, well into Fimbulwinter."

Fimbulwinter: the winter at the end of the world, after the last fuel for the necrosun's accretion disk had been consumed, leaving Earth adrift in orbit around a cold black hole, billions of light-years from anything else. Pierce shivered slightly at the thought of it. "What's the problem with the outside air?"

"We were losing hydrogen too fast, and without hydrogen, there's no water, and without water, we can't maintain a biosphere, and without a biosphere the planet rapidly becomes less habitable—no free oxygen, for one thing. So about thirty billion years ago we deuterated the biosphere as a conservation measure. Of course, that necessitated major adjustments to the enzyme systems of all the life-forms from bacteria on up, and you—and I—are not equipped to run on heavy water; the stuff's toxic to us." Torque pointed at the stream. "You can drink from that, if you like, or order refreshments by phone. But don't drink outside the dome. Don't breathe too much, if you can help it."

Pierce looked around. "So this is basically just a reading room, like a Branch Library. Where's the *real* Library? Where are the archives?"

"You're standing on them." Torque's expression was one of restrained impatience: *Weren't you paying attention in class the day they covered this?* "The plateau this reading room is built on—in fact, the entire upper crust—is riddled with storage cells of memory diamond, beneath a thin crust of sedimentary rock laid down to protect it. We switched the continental-drift cycle off for good about five billion years ago, after the last core cooling cycle. That's when we began accumulating the Library deposits.

"Oh." Pierce looked around. "Well, I suppose I'd better get started. Do you mind?"

"Not at all." Torque turned his back on Pierce and walked away. *"I'll be around if you call me,"* he sent.

Pierce sat down in front of the empty desk and laid his hands palm down on the blotter. *A continent of memory diamond?* The mere idea of that much data beggared the imagination. "It'll be in here somewhere," he muttered, and smiled.

UNHISTORY

ONE OF THE FIRST things that any agent of the Stasis learns is patience. It's not as if they are short of time; their long lives extend beyond the easy reach of memory, and should they avoid death through violence or accident or suicide, they can pursue projects that would exceed the life expectancy of ordinary mortals. And that is how they live in the absence of the principal aspect of their employment, the ability to request access to the timegate.

Pierce thought at first that the vice-chancellor's request would be trivial, a matter of taking a few hours or days to dig down into the stacks and review the historical record. He'd return triumphant, a few minutes upstream of his departure, and present his findings before the council. Xiri would be appropriately adoring, and would doubtless write a series of sonnets about his Library visit (for poetics were in fashion as the densest rational format for sociological-academic case studies in Leng): and his adoptive home time would be spared the rigor and pity of a needless doctrinal war. That was his plan.

It came unglued roughly a week after his arrival, at the point when he stopped flailing around in increasing

----

panic and went for a long walk around the paths of the biome, brooding darkly, trying to quantify the task.

Memory diamond is an astonishingly dense and durable data substrate. It's a lattice of carbon nuclei, like any other diamond save that it is synthetic, and the position of atoms in the lattice represents data. By convention, an atom of carbon 12 represents a zero, and an atom of carbon 13 represents a one; and twelve-point-five grams of memory diamond—one molar weight, a little under half an old-style ounce—stores 6×10^{23} bits of data—or 10^{23} bytes, with compression.

The continent the reading room is situated on is fifteen kilometers thick and covers an area of just under forty million square kilometers, comparable to North and South America combined in the epoch of Pierce's birth. Half of it is memory diamond. There's well over 10^{18} *tons* of the stuff, roughly 10^{23} molar weights. One molar weight of memory diamond is sufficient to hold all the data ever created and stored by the human species prior to Pierce's birth, in what was known at the time as the twenty-first century.

The civilizations over which the Stasis held sway for a trillion years stored a *lot* more data. And when they collapsed, the Stasis looted their Alexandrian archives, binged on stolen data, and vomited it back up at the far end of time.

Pierce's problem was this: more than 90 percent of the Library consisted of lies.

He'd started out, naturally enough, with two pieces of information: the waypoint in his phone that identified the exact location of the porch of his home in Leng, and the designation of the planetary system in M-33 that had aroused such controversy. It was true, as Xiri had said, that the Hegemony was reveling in the feed from the robot exploration fleet that had swept through the Triangulum galaxy tens of millions of years ago. And he knew—he was certain!—that Xiri, and the Hegemony, and the city of Leng with its Mediterranean airs and absurdly scholastic customs existed. He had held her as his wife and lover for nearly two decades-subjective, dwelt there and followed their ways as an honored noble guest for more than ten of those years: he could smell the hot, damp summer evening breeze in his nostrils, the scent of the climbing blue rose vines on the trellis behind his house—

The first time he gave the Library his home address and the identities to search for, it took him to a set of war grave records in the Autonomous Directorate, two years before his first interview with Xiri. He was unamused to note the names of his father- and mother-in-law inscribed in the list of terrorist wreckers and resisters who had been liquidated by the Truth Police in the wake of the liberation of Leng by Directorate forces.

He tried again: this time he was relieved to home in on his return from the field trip to Constantinople— seen through the omnipresent eyes of Xiri's own cams—but was perplexed by her lack of excitement. He backtracked, his search widening out until he discovered to his surprise that according to the Library, the Hegemony was not, in fact, investigating the Triangulum galaxy at all, but focusing on Maffei 1, seven million light-years farther out.

That night he ordered up two bottles of a passable Syrah and drank himself into a solitary stupor for the first time in some years. It was a childish and shortsighted act, but the repeated failures were eating away at his patience. The day after, wiser but somewhat irritable, he tried again, entering his home coordinates into the desk and asking for a view of his hall.

There was no hall, and indeed no Leng, and no Hegemony either; but the angry spear-wielding raccoons had discovered woad.

Pierce stood up, shaking with frustration, and walked out of the reader's cubicle. He stood for a while on the damp green edge of the brook, staring at the play of light across the running water. It wasn't enough. He shed his scholar's robe heedlessly, turned to face the dirt trail that had led him to this dead end, and began to run. Arriving at the entrance airlock, he didn't stop: his legs pounded on, taking him out of the dome and then around it in a long loop, feet thumping on the bony limestone pavement, each plate like the scale of a monstrous fossilized lizard beneath his feet. He kept the glowing dome to his left as he circled it, once, then twice. By the end of the run he was flagging, his chest beginning to burn, the hot, heavy lassitude building in his legs as the sweat dripped down his face.

He slowed to a walk as the airlock came into view again. When he was ready to speak, he activated his phone. *"Torque. Your fucking Library is lying to me. Why is that?"*

"Ah, you've just noticed." Torque sounded amused. *"Come inside and we'll discuss it."*

I don't want to discuss it; I want it to work, Pierce fumed to himself as he trudged back to the airlock. Overhead, three planets twinkled redly across the blind vault of the nighttime sky.

Torque was waiting for him in the clearing, holding a bottle and a pair of shot glasses. "You're going to need this," he said, a twinkle in his eyes. "Everybody does, the first time around."

"Feh." Pierce shuffled stiffly past him, intending to return to the reading cubicle. "What use is a Library full of lies?"

"They're not lies." Torque's response was uncharacteristically mild. "They're unhistory."

"Un—" Pierce stopped dead in his tracks. "There was no unhistory in the Branch Libraries I used," he said tonelessly.

"There wouldn't be. Have you given thought to what happens every time you step through a timegate?"

"Not unduly. What does that have to do with—"

"Everything." Torque allowed a note of irritation to creep into his voice. "You need to pay more attention to theory, Agent. Not all problems can be solved with a knife."

"Huh. So the Library is contaminated with unhistory, because...?"

"*Students.* When you use a timegate, you enter a wormhole, and when you exit from it—well, from the reference frame of your point of emergence, a singularity briefly appears and emits a large gobbet of information. *You.* The information isn't consistent with the time leading up to its sudden appearance—causality may be violated, for one thing, and for another, the information, the traveler, may remember or contain data that wasn't there before. You're just a bundle of data spewed out by a wormhole; you don't have to be consistent with the universe around you. That's how you remember your upbringing and your recruitment, even though nobody else does. Except for the Library."

They came to a clearing and instead of taking the track to the reading room, Torque took a different path.

"Let's suppose you visit a temporal sector—call it A-one—and while you're there, you do something that changes its historical pattern. You're now in sector A-two. A-one no longer exists; it's been overwritten. If there's a Branch Library in A-one, it's now in A-two, and it, too, has changed, because it is consistent with its own history. But the real Library—tell me, how does information enter the Library?"

Pierce floundered. "I thought that was an archival specialty? Every five seconds throughout eternity a listener slot opens for a millisecond, and anything of interest is sent forward to Control."

"Not exactly." Torque stopped on the edge of another clearing in the domed jungle. "The communication slots send data *backward* in time, not forward. There's an epoch almost a billion years long, sitting in the Archaean and Proterozoic eras, where we run the Library relays. The point is—back in the Cryptozoic-relay era, there are no palimpsests. There's no human history to contaminate, nothing there but a bunch of store-and-forward relays. So reports from sector A-one are relayed back to the Cryptozoic, as are reports from sector A-two. And when they're transmitted uptime to the Final Library for compilation, we have two conflicting reports from sector A."

Pierce boggled. "Are you telling me that we don't destroy time lines when we change things? That everything coexists? That's heretical!"

"I'm not preaching heresy." Torque turned to face him. "The sector is indeed overwritten with new history: the other events are unhistory now, stuff that never happened. *Plausible lies.* Raw data that pops out of a wormhole mediated by a naked singularity, if you ask the theorists: causally unconnected with reality. But all the lies end up in the Library. Not only does the Library document all of recorded human history—and there is a *lot* of it, for ubiquitous surveillance technology is both cheap and easy to develop, it's how we define civilization after all—it documents all the possible routes through history that end in the creation of the Final Library. That's why we have the Final Library as well as all the transient, palimpsest-affected Branch Libraries."

It was hard to conceive of. "All right. So the Library is full of internally contradictory time lines. Why can't I find what I'm looking for?"

"Well. If you're using your waypoints correctly, the usual reason why you get a random selection of incorrect views is that someone has rewritten that sector. It's a palimpsest. Not only is the information you came here to seek buried in a near-infinite stack of unhistories, it's unlikely you'll ever be able to return to it—unless you can find the point where that sector's history was altered and undo the alteration."

REPEATEDLY KILLING THE BUDDHA

GRADUATION CEREMONY

YOU WILL AWAKEN EARLY on that day, and you will dress in the formal parade robes of a probationary agent of the Stasis for the last time ever. You have worn these robes many times over the past twenty years, and you are no longer the frightened teenager whose hands held the knife of the aspirant and whose ears accepted their ruthless first order. Had you declined the call, were you still in the era of your birth, you would already be approaching early middle age, the great plague of senescence digging its claws deep beneath your skin; and as it is, even though the medical treatments of the Stasis have given you the appearance of a twenty-five-year-old, your eyes are windows onto the soul of an ancient.

Your mind will be honed as sharp and purposeful as a razor blade, for you will have spent six months preparing for this morning; six months of lonesome despair following Torque's explanation of your predicament, spent in training on the roof of the world, obsessively focused on your final studies. You have completed your internship and your probationary assignments, worked alone and unsupervised in perilous times: now you will present yourself to the examiners to undergo their final and most severe examination, in hope of being accepted at last as an agent of Stasis. As a full agent, you will no longer be limited in your access to the Library: nor will your license to summon timegates be restricted. You will be a trustee, a key-holder in the jailhouse of history, able to rummage through lives on a whim, free to search for what you have lost (or have had taken from you: as yet you are unsure whether it was malice or negligence that destroyed your private life).

You will dress in a saffron robe bound with the black belt of your current rank, and place on your head the beret of an agent-aspirant. Elsewhere in the complex, a dozen other probationers are similarly preparing themselves. You will hang on your belt the dagger that you honed to lethal sharpness the night before, obsessively polishing the symbol of your calling. Before the sun reaches the day's zenith, it will have taken a life: it is your duty to ensure that the victim dies swiftly, painlessly.

Out on the time-weathered flagstones, beneath the deep blue dome of a sky bisected by a glittering torque of orbital-momentum-transfer bodies, you will stand in a row before your teachers and tyrants. Not for the first time, you will find yourself asking if it was all worth it. They will stare down at you and your classmates, ready to pronounce judgment— ready perhaps to admit you to their number as a peer, or to anathematize and cauterize, to unmake and consign into unhistory those who are unworthy. They outnumber your fellow trainees three to one, for they take the training of new eumortals very seriously indeed. They are the eternal guardians of historicity, the arbiters of what really happened. And for no reason you can clearly comprehend, they offered you, you in particular out of a field of a billion contenders, an opportunity.

And there will be speeches. And more speeches. And then Superintendent-of-Scholars Manson will utter a sermon, along exactly the lines one would expect on such an occasion. "This momentous and solemn occasion marks the end of your formal training, but not the end of your studies and your search for excellence. You entered this academy as orphans and strangers, and you shall leave it as agents of the Stasis, sworn to serve our great cause—the total history of the human species." He's going to go on in like vein for nearly an hour, you realize: one homily after another, orthodox ideology personified. Theory before praxis.

"We accept you as you are, human aspirants with human weaknesses and human strengths. We are all human; that is *our* weakness and strength, for we are the agency of human destiny, charged with the holy duty of preserving our species from the triple threat of extinction, transcendental obsolescence, and a cosmos fated to unwind in darkness—notwithstanding your weaknesses, you, brother Chee Yun, with your obsessive exploration of the extremes of pain; you, sister Gretz, with your enthusiasm for the fruit of the dream poppy; you, brother Pierce, with your palimpsest family hobby—we understand all your little vices, and we accept you as you are, despite your weaknesses, despite knowing that only through service to the Stasis will you achieve all that you are destined for—"

You will not bridle angrily when Superintendent-of-Scholars Manson tramples on the grave of your family's unhistory, even though the scars are still raw and weeping, because you know that this is how the ritual unfolds. You will have reviewed the recording delivered in the internal post some days before, heard the breathy rasp of your own voice wavering on the razor edge of horror as he explains the graduation ritual to you-in-the-present. Your fingers will whiten on the sweat-stained leather hilt of your dagger as you await the signal. Though outwardly you remain at peace, inside you will be in turmoil, wondering if you can go through with it. Slaying your grandfather, cutting yourself free from the fabric of history, was one thing; this is something else.

"Stasis demands eternal vigilance, brothers and sisters. It is easier to shape by destruction than to force creation on the boughs of historicity, but we must stand vigilant and ready, if necessary, to intervene even against ourselves should our hands stray from the straightest of strokes. Every time we step from a timegate, we are born anew as information entering the universe from a singularity: we must not allow our hands to be stilled by fear of personal continuity—"

You will realize then that Manson is on track, that he really *is* going to give the order your older self described with shaking voice, and you tense in readiness as you call up a channel to Control, requesting the gate through which you must graduate.

"Weakness is forgivable in one's personal life, but not in the great work. We humans are weak, and sooner or later many of us stray, led into confusion and solipsism by our human grief and hubris. But it is our glory and our privilege that we can change *ourselves*. We do not have to accept a false version of ourselves which have fallen into the errors of wrong thought or despair! Shortly you will be called on to undertake the first of your autosurveillance duties, monitoring your own future self for signs of deviation. Keep a clear head, remember your principles, and be firm in your determination to destroy your own errors: that is all it takes to serve the Stasis well. We are our own best police force, for we can keep track of our own other selves far better than any eternal invigilator." Manson will clap his hands. And then, without further ado, he will add: "You have all been told what it is that you must do in order to graduate. Do it. Prove to me that you have what it takes to be a stalwart pillar of the Stasis. Do it *now*."

You will draw your dagger as your phone sends out the request for a timegate two seconds back in time and a meter behind you. Control acknowledges your request, and you begin to step toward the opening hole in front of you, but as you do so you will sense wrongness, and as you draw breath you will begin to turn, raising your knife to block with a scream forming in the back of your mind: *No! Not me!* But you will be too late. The stranger with your face stepping out of the singularity behind you will tighten his grip on your shoulders, and as you twist your neck to look around, he will use your momentum to aid the edge of the knife you so keenly sharpened. It will whisper through your carotid artery and your trachea, bringing your life to a gurgling, airless fadeout.

The graduation ceremony always concludes this way, with the newly created agents slaughtering their Buddha nature on the stony road beneath the aging stars. It is a pity that you won't be alive to see it in person; it is one of the most profoundly revealing rituals of the time travelers, cutting right to the heart of their existence. But you needn't worry about your imminent death—the other you, born bloody from the singularity that opened behind your back, will regret it as fervently as you ever could.

THE TRIAL

THE DAY AFTER HE murdered himself in cold blood, Agent Pierce received an urgent summons to attend a meeting in the late nineteenth century.

It was, he thought shakily, par for the course: pick an agent, any agent, as long as their home territory was within a millennium or so of the dateline. From Canada in the twenty-first to Germany in the nineteenth, what's the difference? If you were an inspector from the umpty-millionth, it might not look like a lot, he supposed: they were all exuberant egotists, these faceless teeming ur-people who had lived and died before the technologies of total history rudely dispelled the chaos and uncertainty of the pre-Stasis world. And Pierce was a *very* junior agent. Best to see what the inspector wanted.

Kaiserine Germany was not one of Pierce's areas of interest, so he took a subjective month to study for the meeting in advance—basic conversational German, European current events, and a sufficient grounding in late-Victorian London to support his cover as a more than usually adventuresome entrepreneur looking for new products to import—before he stepped out of a timegate in the back of a stall in a public toilet in Spittelmarkt.

Berlin before the century of bombs was no picturesque gingerbread confection: outside the slaughterhouse miasma of the market, the suburbs were dismal narrow-fronted apartment blocks as far as the eye could see, soot-stained by a million brown-coal stoves, the principal olfactory note one of horse shit rather than gasoline fumes (although Rudolf Diesel was even now at work on his engines in a more genteel neighborhood). Pierce departed the public toilet with some alacrity—the elderly attendant seemed to take his emergence as a personal insult—and hastily hailed a cab to the designated meeting place, a hotel in Charlottenberg.

The hotel lobby was close and humid in the summer heat; bluebottles droned around the dark wooden paneling as Pierce looked around for his contact. His phone tugged at his attention as he looked at the inner courtyard, where a cluster of cast-iron chairs and circular tables hinted at the availability of waiter service. Sure enough, a familiar face nodded affably at him.

Pierce approached the table with all the enthusiasm of a condemned man approaching the gallows. "You wanted to see me," he said. There were two goblets of something foamy and green on the table, and two chairs. "Who else?"

"The other drink's for you. Berliner Weiss with Waldmeistersirup. You'll like it. Guaranteed." Kafka gestured at the empty chair. "Sit down."

"How do you know—" *Silly question.* Pierce sat down. "You know this isn't my time?"

"Yes." Kafka picked up a tall, curved glass full of dark brown beer and took a mouthful. "Doesn't matter." He peered at Pierce. "You're a new graduate. Damn,

I don't like this job." He took another mouthful of beer.

"What's happened now?" Pierce asked.

"I don't know. That's why I want you here."

"Is this to do with the time someone tried to assassinate me?"

"No." Kafka shook his head. "It's worse, I'm afraid. One of your tutors may have gone off the reservation. Observation indicated. I'm putting you on the case. You may need—you may need to terminate this one."

"A tutor." Despite himself, Pierce was intrigued. Kafka, the man from Internal Affairs (but his role was unclear, for was it not the case that the Stasis police their own past and future selves?) wanted him to investigate a senior agent and tutor? Ordering him to bug his future self would be understandable, but this—

"Yes." Kafka put his glass down with a curl of his lower lip that bespoke distaste. "We have reason to believe she may be working for the Opposition."

"Opposition." Pierce raised an eyebrow. "There is no opposition—"

"Come, now: don't be naive. *Every* ideology in every recorded history has an opposition. Why should we be any different?"

"But we're—" Pierce paused, the phrase *bigger than history* withering on the tip of his tongue. "Excuse me?"

"Work it through." Kafka was atwitch with barely concealed impatience. "You can't possibly *not* have thought about setting yourself up as a pervert god, can you? Everybody thinks about it, this we know; seed the universe with life, create your own Science Empires, establish a rival interstellar civilization in the deep Cryptozoic, and use it to invade or secede Earth before the Stasis notices—that sort of thing. It's not as if *thinking about it* is a crime: the problems start when an agent far gone in solipsism starts thinking they can do it for real. Or worse, when the Opposition raise their snouts."

"But I—" Pierce stopped, collected his thoughts, and continued. "I thought that never happened? That the self-policing thing was a…an adequate safeguard?"

"Lad." Kafka shook his head. "You clearly mean well. And self-policing does indeed work adequately most of the time. But don't let the security theater at your graduation deceive you: there are failure modes. We set you a large number of surveillance assignments to muddy the water—palimpsests all, of course, we overwrite them once they deliver their reports so that future-you retains no memory of them—but you can't watch yourself all the time. And there are administrative errors. You're not only the best monitor of your own behavior, but the best-placed individual to know how best to corrupt you. We are human and imperfect, which is why we need an external Internal Affairs department. Someone has to coordinate things, especially when the Opposition are involved."

"The Opposition?" Pierce picked up his glass and drank deeply, studying Kafka. "Who are they?"

Who do you want me to rat out? he wondered. *Myself?* Surely Kafka couldn't have overlooked his history with Xiri, now buried beneath the dusty pages of a myriad of rewrites?

"You'll know them when you meet them." Kafka emitted a little mirthless chuckle and stood up. "Come upstairs to my office, and I'll show you why I requested you for this assignment."

Kafka's office occupied the entire top floor of the building and was reached by means of a creaking mesh-fronted elevator that rose laboriously through the well of a wide staircase. It was warm, but not obnoxiously so, as Pierce followed Kafka out of the elevator cage. "The door is reactive," Kafka warned, placing a protective hand on the knob. Hidden glands were waiting beneath a patina of simulated brass, ready to envenomate the palm of an unwary intruder. "Door: accept Agent Pierce. General defenses: accept Agent Pierce with standard agent privilege set. You may follow me now."

Kafka opened the door wide. Beyond it, ranks of angled wooden writing desks spanned the room from wall to wall. A dark-suited iteration of Kafka perched atop a high stool behind each one of them, pens moving incessantly across their ledgers. A primitive visitor (one not slain on the spot by the door handle, or the floor, or the wallpaper) might have gaped at the ever-changing handwriting and spidery diagrams that flickered on the pages, mutating from moment to moment as the history books redrew themselves, and speculated about digital paper. Pierce, no longer a primitive, felt the hair under his collar rise as he polled his phone, pulling up the number of rewrites going on in the room. "You're really working Control hard," he said in the direction of Kafka's receding back.

"This is the main coordination node for prehistoric Germany." Kafka tucked his hands behind his back as he walked, stoop-shouldered, between desks. "We're close enough to the start of Stasis history to make meddling tricky—we have to keep track of continuity, we can't simply edit at will." Meddling with prehistory, before the establishment of the ubiquitous monitoring and recording technologies that ultimately fed the Library at the end of time, ought to be risk-free: if a Neolithic barbarian froze to death on a glacier, unrecorded, the implications for deep history were trivial. But the rules were fluid, and interference was risky: if a time traveler were to shoot the Kaiser, for example, or otherwise derail the ur-history line leading up to the Stasis, it could turn the entire future into a palimpsest. "The individual I am investigating is showing an unhealthy interest in the phase boundary between Stasis and prehistory."

One of the deskbound Kafkas looked up, his eyebrows furrowing with irritation. "Could you take this somewhere else?" he asked.

"I'm sorry," Pierce's Kafka replied with abrupt humility. "Agent Pierce, this way."

As Kafka led Pierce into an office furnished like an actuary's hermitage, Pierce asked, "Aren't you at risk of anachronism yourselves? Multitasking like that, so close to the real Kafka's datum?"

Kafka smiled sepulchrally as he sat down behind the heavy oak desk. "I take precautions. And the fewer individuals who know what's in those ledgers, the better." He gestured at a small, hard seat in front of it. "Be seated, Agent Pierce. Now, in your own words. Tell me about your relationship with Agent-Scholar Yarrow. *Everything*, if you please." He reached into his desk drawer and withdrew a smart pad. "I have a transcript of your written correspondence here. We'll go through it line by line next..."

Funeral in Berlin

THE INTERROGATION LASTED THREE days. Kafka didn't even bother to erase it from Pierce's time line retroactively: clearly he was making a point about the unwisdom of crossing Internal Affairs.

Afterward, Pierce left the hotel and wandered the streets of Berlin in a neurasthenic daze.

Does Kafka trust me? Or not? On balance, probably not: the methodical, calm grilling he'd received, the interrogation about the precise meaning of Yarrow's love letters (faded memories from decades ago, to Pierce's mind), had been humiliating, an emotional strip search. Knowing that Kafka understood his dalliance with Yarrow as a youthful indiscretion, knowing that Kafka clearly knew of (and tolerated) his increasingly desperate search for the point at which his history with Xiri had been overwritten, only made it worse. *We can erase everything that gives meaning to your life if we feel like it.* Feeling powerless was a new and shocking experience for Pierce, who had known the freedom of the ages: a return to his pre-Stasis life, half-starved and skulking frightened in the shadows of interesting times.

And then there was the incipient paranoia that any encounter with Internal Affairs engendered. *Am I being watched right now?* he wondered as he walked. *A ghost-me surveillance officer working for Internal Affairs, or something else?* Kafka would be mad not to assign him a watcher, he decided. If Yarrow was under investigation, then he himself must be under suspicion. Guilt by association was the first rule of counter-espionage, after all.

A soul-blighting sense of depression settled into his bones. He'd had an inkling of it for months, ever since his increasingly frantic search in the Library, but Kafka's quietly pedantic examination had somehow catalyzed a growing certainty that he would never see Xiri, or Magnus and Liann, ever again—that if he could ever find them, shadows cast from his mind by the merciless inspection-lamp glare of Internal Affairs would banish them farther into unhistory.

Therefore, he wandered.

Civilization lay like a heavy blanket upon the land, rucked up in gray-faced five-story apartment

blocks and pompous stone-faced business establish-
ments, their pillars and porticoes and cornicework
swollen with self-importance like so many amorous
street pigeons. The city sweated in the summer heat,
the stench and flies of horse manure in the streets
contributing a sour pungency to the sharp stink of
stove smoke.

Other people shared the Strasse with him; here a
peddler selling apples from a handcart, there a couple
taking the air together. Pierce walked slowly along the
sidewalk of a broad street, sweating in his suit and taking what shelter he could from the merciless summer
sun beneath the awnings of shops, letting his phone's
navigation aid guide his footsteps even as he wondered
despondently if he would ever find his way home. He
could wander through the shadowy world of historicity forever, never finding his feet—for though the
Stasis and their carefully cultivated tools of ubiquitous
monitoring had nailed down the sequence of events
that comprised history, history was a tangled weave,
many threads superimposed and redyed and snipped
out of the final pattern...

The scent was his first clue that he was not alone,
floral and sweet and tickling the edge of his nostrils
with a half-remembered sense of illicit excitement that
made his heart hammer. The shifting sands of memory
gave way: *I know that smell—*

His phone vibrated. *"Show no awareness,"* someone
whispered inside his skull in Urem. *"They are watching
you."* The voice was his own.

The strolling couple taking the air arm in arm were ahead of him. It was *her* scent, the familiar bouquet, but—"*Where are you?*" he sent. "*Show yourself.*"

The phone buzzed again like an angry wasp trapped inside his ribs. "*Not with watchers. Go to this location and wait,*" said the traitor voice, as a spatial tag nudged the corner of his mind. "*We'll pick you up.*" The rendezvous was a couple of kilometers away, in a public park notorious by night: a French-letter drop for a dead-letter drop.

He tried not to stare. *It* might *be her,* he thought, trying to shake thirty-year-old jigsaw memories into something that matched a glimpse of a receding back in late-nineteenth-century dress and broad-brimmed hat. He turned a corner in his head even as they turned aside into a residential street: "*Internal Affairs just interrogated me about Yarrow.*"

"*You told us already. Go now. Leave the rest to us.*"

Pierce's phone fell silent. He glanced sideways out of the corners of his eyes, but the strolling couple were no longer visible. He sniffed, flaring his nostrils in search of an echo of that familiar scent, but it, too, was gone. Doubtless they'd never been here at all; they were Stasis, after all. Weren't they?

Guided by his phone's internal nudging, Pierce ambled slowly toward the park, shoulders relaxed and hands clasped behind his back as if enjoying a quiet afternoon stroll. But his heart was pounding and there was an unquiet sensation in the pit of his stomach, as if he harbored a live grenade in his belly. *You told*

us already. Go now. Leave the rest to us. His own traitor voice implying lethally spiraling cynicism. *They
are watching you.* The words of a self-crowned pervert god, hubris trying to dam the flow of history;
or the mysterious Opposition that Kafka had warned
him of? It was imponderable, intolerable. *I could be
walking into a trap,* Pierce considered the idea, and
immediately began to activate a library of macros in
his phone that he'd written for such eventualities. As
Superintendent-of-Scholars Manson had ceaselessly
reminded him, a healthy paranoia was key to avoiding further encounters with cardiac leeches and less
pleasant medical interventions.

Pierce crossed the street and walked beside a canal
for a couple of blocks, then across a bridge and toward
the tree-lined gates of a park. Possibilities hummed
in the dappled shadows of the grass like a myriad of
butterfly wings broken underfoot, whispering on the
edge of actuality like distant thunder. This part of history, a century and more before the emergence of the
first universal-surveillance society, before the beginning of the history to which the Stasis laid claim, was
mutable in small but significant ways. Nobody could
say for sure who might pass down any given street in
any specified minute, and deem it disruptive: the lack
of determinism lent a certain flexibility to his options.

Triggering one of his macros as he stepped through
the gate to the park, between one step and the next
Pierce walked through a storeroom in the basement of
a Stasis station that had been dust and ruins a billion

years before the ice sheets retreated from the North German plains. It had lain disused for a century or so when he entered it, and nobody else would use it for at least a decade thereafter—he'd set monitors, patient trip wires to secure his safe time. He tarried there for almost three hours, picking items from a well-stocked shelf and sending out messages to order them from a factory on a continent that didn't yet exist, eating a cold meal from a long-storage ration pack, and trying to regain his emotional balance in time for the meeting that lay ahead.

An observer close on his tail would have seen a flicker; when he completed the stride his suit was heavier, the fabric stiffer to the touch, and his shoulders slightly stooped beneath the weight concealed within. There were other changes, some of them internal. Perhaps the observers would see, but: *Leave the rest to us.* He slipped his hands into his pockets, blinked until the itching subsided and the heads-up display settled into place across the landscape, scanning and amplifying. He had summoned watchers, circling overland: invisible and silent, nerves connected to his center. *Fuck Kafka's little game,* he thought furiously. *Fuck them all.* Three hours in his unrecorded storeroom in the Cryptozoic had given him time for his depression to ferment into anger. *I want answers!*

It was a hot day, and the park was far from empty. There were young women, governesses or maids, pushing the prams of their bourgeois employers; clerks or office workers skipping work and some juvenile ne'er-do-wells playing truant from the gymnasium; here a street sweeper and there a dodgy character with a barrel organ and behind him a couple of vagrants sharing a bottle of schnapps. At the center of a well-manicured lawn, an ornate stone pedestal supported a clock with four brass faces. Pierce, letting his phone drive his feet, casually glanced around while his threat detector scanned through the chaff. *Nobody*— His phone buzzed again.

"What was the tavern where you fell for me called?" An achingly familiar voice whispered in his ear.

"Something to do with wildfowl, in Carnegra, the Red Goose or Red Duck or something like that—"

"Hard contact in three seconds," his own voice interrupted from nowhere. *"Button up and hit the ground on my word. Now."*

Pierce dived toward the grassy strip beside the path as flaring crimson threat markers appeared all around him. As he fell, his suit bloated and darkened: rubbery cones expanded like a frightened hedgehog's quills as his collar expanded and rotated, hooding him. In the space of a second the park's population doubled, angular metallic figures flickering into being all around. Time flickered and strobed as timegates snapped open and shut, expelling sinister cargo. Pierce twitched ghost muscles convulsively, triggering camouflage routines as the incoming drones locked onto each other and spat missiles and laser fire.

"What's going on?"

"Palimpsest ambush! Hard..."

The signal stuttered into silence, hammered flat by jammers and raw, random interference. Pierce began to roll, rising to sit as his suit's countermeasures flared. *This is crazy,* he thought, shocked by the violence of the attack. *They can't hope to conceal—*

The sky turned violet-white, the color of lightning: the grass around him began to smoke.

The temperature rose rapidly. His suit was just beginning to char from the prompt radiation pulse as the ground opened under him, toppling him backward into darkness.

REDUX

Army of You

When you see the ground swallow Pierce you will breathe a sigh of relief—you'll finally have the luxury of knowing that one of your iterations has made it out of death ground. But the situation will be too deadly to give you respite. If Internal Affairs are willing to *start* with combat drones and orbital X-ray lasers, then escalate from there, where will they stop? How badly do they want you?

Very badly, it seems.

There's going to be hell to pay when it's time for the cleanup; ur-history doesn't have room for a nuclear blitzkrieg on the capital of the Second Reich. The calcinated, rapidly skeletonizing remains of the governesses and the organ grinders contort and burst in the searing wind from the Hiroshima miscarriage, and the four faces of the clock glow cherry red and slump to the ground as a dozen more of you flicker into view, anonymous in their heat-flash-silvered battle armor. The echo-armies of your combat drones fan out all around, furiously dumping heat through transient timegates into the cryogenic depths of the far future as they exchange fire with the enemy's soldiers. *"Extraction complete. Prepare to move out,"* says your phone; the iteration tag of that version of you is astronomical, in the millions. This isn't just a palimpsest ambush: it's an entire talmud of rewrites and commentaries and attempted paradoxes piled up in a threatening tsunami of unhistory and dumped on your heads.

You'll grab your future self's metadata and jump toward a timegate to a dispersal zone drifting high in orbit above ruddy Jupiter's north pole, nearly a billion years in the future: the rocket motors at your suit's shoulders and ankles kick hard, and as you loft, you'll catch a flashing glimpse of the Mach wave from the first heat strike surging outward, lifting and crumpling schools and hospitals and churches and apartments and houses and shops in the iron name of Internal Affairs.

They won't find this dispersal zone. They won't uncover the truth about Control, either, or about the Opposition—you'll be sure of that for as long as you continue to live and breathe.

You will look down, between your feet, at the swirling orange-and-cream chaos of Jupiter's upper atmosphere. Your armor will ping and tick quietly as

---

it cools, and you will wait while the star trackers get a fix on your position, your mind empty of everything but a quiet satisfaction, the reward for a job well-done: the extraction of your cardinal iterant from the grasp of Internal Affairs. Somewhere else in time—millions of years ago—the rewrite war is still going on, the virtual legions of you playing a desperate shell game with Kafka: but you've won. All that's left to do is to deftly insert the zombie ringer into ur-history on his way into Kafka's court, primed to tell Internal Affairs exactly what you want them to know, then to orchestrate a drawdown and withdrawal from the ruins of Berlin before Kafka overwrites the battle zone and restores the proper flow of history.

Your suit will beep quietly for attention. "Scan complete," it announces. "Acceleration commencing." The thrusters will push briefly, reorienting you, sliding Jupiter out of sight behind your back. And then the rockets will kick in again, pushing you toward the yard, and the fleet of thirty-kilometer-long starships abuilding, and Yarrow.

HE GOT YOUR GIRL

I'M ALIVE, THOUGHT PIERCE, then did a double take. *I'm alive?* Everything was black, and he couldn't tell which way was up. There was a metallic taste in his mouth, and he ached everywhere.

"Where am I?" he asked.

"You'll have to wait while we cut you out of that," said a stranger. Their voice sounded oddly muffled, and he realized with surprise that it wasn't coming from inside him. "You took an EMP that fried your suit. You only just made it out in time—you took several sieverts. We've got a bed waiting for you."

Something pushed at his side, and he felt a strange tipping motion. "Am I in free fall?" he asked.

"Of course. Try not to move."

I'm not on Earth, he realized. It was strange; he'd effectively visited hundreds of planets with ever-shifting continents and biospheres, but he'd never been off Earth before. They were all aspects of Gaia, causally entangled slices through the set of all possible Earths that the Stasis called their own.

Someone tugged on his left foot, and he felt a chill of cold air against his skin. His toes twitched. "That's very good, keep doing that. Tell me if anything hurts." The voice was still muffled by the remains of his hood, but he could place it now. Kari, a quiet woman, one of the trainees from the class above him. He tensed, panic rising in a choking wave. "Hey—Yarrow! He's stressing out—"

"Hold still, Pierce." Yarrow's voice in his ears, also fuzzy. "Your phone's off-line; it took a hit too. Kari's with us. It's going to be all right."

You don't have any right to tell me that, he thought indignantly, but the sound of her voice had the desired effect. *So Kari's one of them too.* Was there no end to the internal rot within the Stasis? In all honesty, considering his own concupiscence—possibly not. He tried to slow his breathing, but it was slowly getting stuffy and hot inside the wreckage of his survival suit.

More parts detached themselves from his skin. He was beginning to itch furiously, and the lack of gravity seemed to be making him nauseous. Finally, the front of his hood cracked open and floated away. He blinked teary eyes against the glare, trying to make sense of what his eyes were telling him.

"Kari—"

The spherical drone floating before his face wore her face on its smartskin. A flock of gunmetal lampreys swam busily behind it, worrying at pieces of the dead and mildly radioactive suit. Some distance beyond, a wall of dull blue triangles curved around him, dishlike, holes piercing it in several places.

"Try not to speak," said Kari's drone. "You've taken a borderline-fatal dose, and we're going to have to get you to a sick bay right away."

His throat ached. "Is Yarrow there?"

Another spherical drone floated into view from somewhere behind him. It wore Xiri's face. "My love? I'll visit you as soon as you've cleared decontamination. The enemy are always trying to sneak bugs in: they wouldn't let me through to see you now. Be strong, my lord." She smiled, but the worry-wrinkles at the corners of her eyes betrayed her. "I'm very proud of you."

He tried to reply, but his stomach had other ideas and attempted to rebel. "Feel. Sick…"

Someone kissed the back of his neck with lips of silver, and the world faded out.

Pierce regained consciousness with an abrupt sense of rupture, as if no time at all had passed: someone had switched his sense of awareness off and on again, just as his parents might once have power-cycled a balky appliance.

"Love? Pierce?"

He opened his eyes and stared at her for a few seconds, then cleared his throat. It felt oddly normal: the aches had all evaporated. "We've got to stop meeting like this." The bed began to rise behind his back. "Xiri?"

Her clothing was outrageous to Hegemonic forms (not to say anachronistic or unrevealing), but she was definitely his Xiri; as she leaned forward and hugged him fiercely he felt something bend inside him, a dam of despair crumbling before a tidal wave of relief. "How did they find you?" he asked her shoulder, secure in her embrace. "*Why* did they reinstate—"

"Hush. Pierce. You were so ill—"

He hugged her back. "I was?"

"They kept me from you for half a moon! And the burns, when they cut that suit away from you. What did you *do*?"

Pierce pondered the question. "I changed my mind about...something I'd agreed to do..."

They lay together on the bed until curiosity got the better of him. "Where are we? When are we?" *Where did you get that jumpsuit?*

Xiri sighed, then snuggled closer to him. "It's a long story," she said quietly. "I'm still not sure it's true."

"It must be, now," he pointed out reasonably, "but perhaps it wasn't, for a while. But where are we?"

She eased back a little. "We're in orbit around Jupiter. But not for much longer."

"But I—" He stopped. "Really?"

"They disconnected your phone, or I could show you. The colony fleets, the shipyards."

He blinked at her, astonished. "How?"

"We all have phone implants, here." Her eyes sparkled with amusement. "This isn't the Stasis you know."

"I'd guessed." He swallowed. "How long has it been for you?"

"Since"—her breath caught, a little ragged—"two years. A little longer."

He gently trapped her right hand in his, ran his thumb across the smooth, plump skin on the back of her wrist. She let him. "Almost the same." He swallowed once more. "I thought I'd never see you again. Anyone would think they'd planned this."

"Oh, but they did." She gave a nervous little laugh. "He said they didn't want us to, to desynchronize. Get too far apart." Her fingers closed around his thumb, constricting and warm.

"Who is 'he'?" asked Pierce, although he thought he knew.

"He used to be you, once. That's what he told me." Her grip tightened suddenly. "He's not you, love. It's not the same. *At all.*"

"I must see him."

Pierce tried to sit up: Xiri clung to him, dragging him down. "No! Not yet," she hissed.

Pierce stopped struggling before he hurt her. His arms and his stomach muscles felt curiously strong, almost as if they'd never been damaged. "Why not?"

"Scholar Yarrow asked me to, to intercede. She said you'd want to confront him." She tensed when she spoke Yarrow's name. "She was right. About lots of things."

"What's her position here?"

"She's with him." Xiri hesitated. "It took much getting used to. I made a fool of myself once, early on."

He raised a hand to stroke her hair. "I can understand that." Pierce pondered his lack of reaction. "It's been years since I knew her, you know. And if he's who—what—I think he is, he was never married to you. Was he?"

"No." She lay against him in silence for a while. "What are you going to do?" she asked in a small voice.

Pierce smiled at the ceiling. (It was low, and bare of decoration: another sign, if he needed one, that he was not back in the Hegemony.) For the time being, the shock and joy of finding her again had left him giddy with relief. "Where are the children?" he asked, forcing himself: one last test.

"I left Liann with a nurse. Magnus is away, in the ship's scholasticos." Concern slowly percolated across her expression. "They've grown a lot: do you think—"

He breathed out slowly, relieved. "There will be time to get to know them again, yes." She reached over his chest and hugged him tight. He stroked her hair, content for the moment but sadly aware that everything was about to change. "But tell me one thing. What is it that you're so desperate to keep from me?"

Nation of Me

"GOOD TO SEE YOU, Pierce," said the man on the throne. He smiled pleasantly but distantly. "I gather you've been keeping well."

Pierce had already come to understand that the truly ancient were not like ordinary humans. "Do you remember being me?" he asked, staring.

The man on the throne raised an eyebrow. "Wouldn't you like to know?" He gestured at the bridge connecting his command dais to the far side of the room. "You may approach." Combat drones and uniformed retainers withdrew respectfully, giving Pierce a wide berth.

He tried not to look down as he walked across the bridge, with only partial success. The storms of Jupiter swirled madly beneath his feet. It had made him nauseous the first time he'd seen them, through a dumb-glass window aboard the low-gee shuttle that had brought him hence—evidently his captors wanted to leave him in no doubt that he was a long way from home. Occulting the view of the planet was the blue-tinged quicksilver disk of the largest timegate he'd ever seen, holding open in defiance of protocol with preposterous, scandalous persistence.

"Why am I here?" Pierce demanded.

A snort. "Why do you think?"

"You're me." Pierce shrugged. "Me with a whole lot more experience and age, and an attitude problem." They'd dressed him in the formal parade robes of a Stasis agent rather than the black jumpsuits that seemed to be de rigueur around this place. It was a petty move, to enforce his alienation: and besides, it had no pockets. To fight back, he focused on the absurd. Black jumpsuits and shiny boots, on a space-ship? Someone around here clearly harbored thespian fantasies. "And now you've got me."

His older self stiffened. "We need to talk alone." His eyes scanned the throne room. "You lot: dismissed."

Pierce glanced round just in time to see the last of the human audience flicker into unhistory. He looked back toward the throne. "I was hoping we could keep this civilized," he said mildly. "You've got all the lever-age you need. I'm in your power." *There*: it was out in the open. Not that there'd been any doubt about it, even from the beginning. This ruthless ancient with his well-known mirror-face and feigned bonhomie had made Pierce's position crystal clear with his choice of greeters. All that was left was for Pierce to politely bare his throat and hope for a favorable outcome.

"I didn't rescue you from those scum in order to throw you away again"—his older self seemed almost irritated—"though what you see in *her*..." He shook his head. "You're safe here."

Pierce rolled his eyes. "Oh, really. And I suppose if I decline to go along with whatever little proposition you're about to put to me, you'll just let me walk away, is that it? Rather than, oh, rewind the audience and try again with a clean-sheet me?" He met the even gaze of the man in the throne and suddenly felt finger high.

"No," said the man on the throne, after a momentary pause. "That won't be necessary. I'm not going to ask you to do anything you wouldn't ask me to let you do."

"Oh." Pierce considered this for a moment. "You're with the Opposition, though. Aren't you? And you know I'm not." Honesty made him add, "Yet."

"I told you he'd say that," said Yarrow, behind him. Pierce's head whipped round. She nodded at him, but kept her smile for the man on the throne. "He's young and naive. Go easy on him."

The man on the throne nodded. "He's not *that* naive, my lady." He frowned. "Pierce, you slit the throat of your own double, separated from you by seconds. You joined the Stasis, after all. But do you really imagine it gets easier with age, when you've had time to meditate on what you've done? There's a reason why armies send the flower of their youth to do the killing and dying, not the aged and cynical.

We have a name for those who find murder gets easier with experience: 'monsters.' "

He raised a hand. "Chairs all around." A pair of seats appeared on the dais, facing him: ghosts of carved diamond, fit for the lords of creation. "I think you should be the one to tell him the news," he suggested to Yarrow. "I'm not sure he'd believe me. He hasn't had time to recover from the trauma yet."

"All right." Yarrow slid gratefully into her own chair, then glanced at Pierce. "You'd better sit down."

"Why?" Pierce lowered himself into his seat expectantly.

"Because"—she nodded at Pierce's elder self, who returned the nod with a drily amused smile—"he's not just a member of the Opposition: he's our leader. That's why Internal Affairs have been all over you like ants. And that's why we had to extract you and bring you here."

"Rubbish." Pierce crossed his arms. "That's not why you had to grab me. You've already got him: I assume I'm a palimpsest or leftover from an assassination attempt. So what do you want with *me*? In the here and now, I mean?"

Yarrow looked flustered. "Pierce—"

His older self placed a restraining hand on her knee as he leaned forward. "Allow me?" He looked Pierce in the eyes. "The Opposition is not—you probably already worked this out—external to the Stasis; we come from within. The Stasis is broken, Pierce. It's drifting rudderless toward the end of time. We've got a...an alternative plan for survival. Internal Affairs is tasked with maintaining internal standards; they're opposed to structural change at all costs. They overwrote your wife's epoch because they discovered possible evidence of our success."

The evidence of abandoned cities on an alien moon, the fleet of gigantic slower-than-light colony starships—was this all just internal politics within the Stasis hierarchy?

"Whatever would they want to do that for?" he asked. "They're not interested in deep space." Except insofar as there were threats to the survival of humanity that had to be dealt with.

Yarrow shook her head. "We disagree. They're *very* interested in deep space—specifically, in keeping us out of it." She inhaled deeply. "Did you notice, when you were consulting the Library, any sign of histories that touched on extraterrestrial settlement? Even though we have reterraformed the Earth thousands of times over, strip-mined the sun, rearranged gas giants, built black holes, and ripped an entire star system from its native galactic cluster?" Pierce shook his head, uncertain. "We've built and destroyed thousands of biospheres, sculpted continents, we outnumber the stars in the cosmos—but we've never spread to other solar systems! Doesn't that strike you as a little odd?"

"But we coevolved with our planet; we're not adapted to life elsewhere—" Pierce stopped. *We can do terraforming, and timegates,* he realized. *Even if we can only have one wormhole end open at any given time.*

115

We rebuilt the sun. *We've mapped every planet within ten million light-years.* "Are we?" he asked, plaintively.

"There's a Science Empire running down on Earth right now," said the man on the throne. "They've been studying that question for twelve thousand years. We brought them the probe fleet reports. They say it can be done, and they've been building and launching a colony ship a year for the past six centuries." He frowned. "We've had that big gate in place ever since the dawn of civilization, to block Internal Affairs from detecting and overwriting our operation here. Officially we're in the middle of a fallow epoch, and the system should be uninhabited and uninhabitable: we moved in ahead of the first scheduled Reseeding. But they never give up. Sooner or later they'll notice us and start looking for the other side of our barricade, the static drop we funneled you through."

"What happens when they find it?" asked Pierce.

"Six hundred inhabited worlds die, and that's just for starters," Yarrow said quietly. "Call it unhistory if you like euphemisms—but did your graduation kill feel unreal to you? Unlike your"—her nose wrinkled in the ghost of a sniff—"wife and children, the inhabitants of the colony worlds won't be retrievable through the Library."

"And those six hundred planets are just the seed corn," his older self chimed in. "The start of something vast."

"But why?" he asked. "Why would they...?" He stopped.

"The Stasis isn't about historicity," said Yarrow. "That might be the organization's raison d'être, but the raw truth of the matter is that the Stasis is about *power*. Like any organization, it lives and grows for itself, not for the task with which it is charged. The governing committee—it's very sad. But it's been like this as long as there's been a Stasis."

"We rescued you because we specifically want you—my first iteration, or as near to it as we've been able to get, give or take the assassination ambush in Carnegra," said the man on the throne. "We need your help to cut us free from the dead hand of history."

"But what—" Pierce lowered his hands to touch his belly. "My phone," he said slowly. "It's damaged, but you could have repaired it. It's not there anymore, is it?"

Yarrow nodded slowly. "Can you tell me why?" she asked.

RESEEDING

A Brief Alternate History of the Universe

Slide 1.

Our solar system under the Stasis, first epoch.

Continents slide and drift, scurrying and scraping across the surface of the mantle. Lights flicker around the coastlines, strobing on and off in kiloyear cycles as civilizations rise and fall. In space, the swarm of orbital-momentum-transfer robots built from the bones of Ceres begin to cycle in and out, slowly pumping energy downwell to the Earth to drag it farther from the slowly brightening sun.

S<small>LIDE</small> 2.

Snapshot: something unusual is happening.

We zoom in on a ten-thousand-year slice, an eyeblink flicker of geological time. For millions of years beforehand, the Earth was quiet, its continents fallen dark in the wake of a huge burping hiccup of magma that flooded from the junction of the Cocos and Nazca continental plates. But now the lights are back, jewels sprinkled across the nighttime hemispheres of unfamiliar continents. Unusually, they aren't confined to the surface—three diamond necklaces ring the planet in glory, girdling the equator in geosynchronous orbit. And floating beyond them, at the L1 Lagrange point betwixt Earth and Luna, sits the anomalous glowing maw of an unusually large timegate.

The natives appear to be restless...

S<small>LIDE</small> 3.

A slow slide of viewpoint out to Jupiter orbit shows that the anomaly is spreading. Already some of the smaller Jovian moons are missing; Thebe and Amalthea have vanished, and something appears to be *eating* Himalea. A metallic cloud of smaller objects swarms in orbit around Europa, pinpricks of light speckling their surface.

Meanwhile, the shoals of momentum-transfer bodies are thinning, their simple design replaced by numerous perversions of form and purpose. Still powered by light sails, the new vehicles carry exotic machines for harvesting energy from the solar wind and storing it as antimatter. Shuttles move among them like ants amidst an aphid farm, harvesting and storing their largesse as they swing out to Jupiter before dropping back in toward Mercury.

Some of the hundreds of metal moons that orbit Europa are glowing at infrared wavelengths, their temperature suspiciously close to three hundred degrees Kelvin. Against the planetary measure of the solar system they are tiny—little bigger than the moons of Mars. But they're among the largest engineered structures ever built by the dreaming apes; vaster than cities and more massive than pyramids. And soon they will start to move.

SLIDE 4.

Three thousand years pass.

Earth lies dark and unpopulated once more, for humanity—as always—has gone extinct. Of the great works in Jupiter orbit few traces remain. The great ships have gone, the shipyards have long since been deorbited into the swirling chaos of the gas giant's atmosphere, and the malformed, warped transfer bodies have been cannibalized and restored to their original purpose.

Five small moons have disappeared, and slowly healing gouges show the sites of huge mining works on Io and Europa, but by the time the Stasis reseed Earth (two-thirds of a million years hence) even the slow resurfacing of Europa's icy caul will have obscured the signs of industry. It may be thousands of years after that before anybody notices.

SLIDE 5.

Twenty million years pass, and the galaxy slowly lights up with a glare of coherent light, waste energy from the communications traffic between the inhabited worlds.

The first generation colonies have long since guttered into senescence and extinction; so have the third and fourth generations. Of the first generation, barely one in five prospered—but that was sufficient. Those that live spawn prolifically. Planets are common, rocky terrestrial bodies far from rare, and even some of the more exotic types (water giants, tide-locked rocky giants in orbit around red dwarfs, and others) are amenable to human purpose. Where no planets are available, life is harder, prone to sudden extinction events: nobody survives the collapse of civilization aboard a space colony. But the tools and technologies of terraforming are well-known, and best practice, of a kind, develops. Many of the dwellers have adapted to their new habitats so well that they're barely recognizable as primates anymore, or even mammals.

SLIDE 6.

Three billion years pass.

Two huge, glittering clouds of sentience fall through each other, a magnificently coordinated fly-past of fleets of worlds meshing across the endless void. Shock waves thunder through the gas clouds, and millions of massive, short-lived new stars ignite and detonate like firecrackers. The starburst is indeed enormous. But for the most part, the inhabited worlds are safe: swarms of momentum-transfer robots, their numbers uncountable, work for millions of years ahead of and behind the event to direct the closest encounters. Emergent flocking rules and careful plans laid far in advance have steered colonies clear of the high-risk territories, marshaling brown dwarfs as dampers and buffers to redirect the tearaway suns—and both galaxies are talking to each other, for the expanding sphere of sentience now encompasses the entire Local Group.

Earth is no longer inhabited in this epoch; but the precious timegate remains, an oracular hub embedded in a cluster of exotic artificial worlds, conducting and orchestrating the dance of worlds.

There are now a hundred million civilizations within the expanding bubble of intelligence, each with an average population of billions. They are already within an order of magnitude of the Stasis's ultimate population, and they are barely a thousandth of its age. The universe, it appears, has started to wake up.

SLIDE 7.

The crystal ball is clouded...

THE KINDEST LIES

THEY WALKED ALONG A twisting path between walls of shrubs and creepers, and a few short trees, growing from mounds of damp-smelling soil. The path appeared to be of old sandstone, shot through with seams of a milky rock like calcite: appearances were deceptive.

"You played me like a flute," said Pierce. He held his hands behind his back, as was his wont, keeping an arm's reach aside from her.

"I did not!" Her denial was more in hurt than in anger. "I didn't know about this until he—you—recruited me." Her boot scuffed a rock leaning like a rotten tooth from the side of a herbaceous border: tiny insects scuttled from her toes, unnoticed. "I was still in training. Like you, when you were tapped for, for other things."

They walked in silence for a minute, uphill and around a winding corner, then down a flight of steps cut into the side of a low hill.

"If this is all simply an internal adjustment, why doesn't Internal Affairs shut everything down?" he asked. "They must know who is involved..."

"They don't." She shook her head. "When you call in a request for a timegate, your phone doesn't say, 'By the way, this iteration of Pierce is a member of the Opposition.' All of us were compliant—once. If they catch us, they can backtrack along our history and undo the circumstances that led to our descent into dissidence; and sometimes we can catch and isolate *them*, put them in an environment where doubt flourishes. If they started unmaking every agent suspected of harboring disloyal thoughts, it would trigger a witch hunt that would tear Stasis apart: we're not the kind who'd go quietly. Hence their insistence on control, alienation from family and other fixed reference points, complicity in shared atrocity. They aim to stifle disloyal thoughts before the first germination."

"Huh." They came to a fork in the path. A stone bench, stained gray and gently eroded by lichen, sat to one side. "Were you behind the assassination attempt, then?"

"No." She perched tentatively at one side of the bench. "That was definitely Internal Affairs. They were after him, not you."

"Him—"

"The iteration of you that never stayed in the Hegemony, never met Xiri, eventually drifted into different thoughts and met Yarrow again under favorable circumstances—"

Pierce slowly turned around as she was speaking, but in every direction he looked there was no horizon, just a neatly landscaped wall of mazes curving gently toward the zenith. "It seems to me that they're out of control."

"Yes." She became intent, focused, showing him her lecturer's face. "All organizations that are founded for a purpose rapidly fill with people who see their role as an end in itself. Internal Affairs are a secondary growth. If they ever succeed, there won't be anything left of the Stasis but Internal Affairs, everyone spying on themselves for eternity and a day, trying to preserve a single outcome without allowing anyone to ask why..."

Not everything added up. Still thinking, Pierce sat down gingerly at the other side of the bench. Not looking at her, he said: "I met Imad and Leila, Xiri's parents. How could they have survived? Everyone kills their own grandparents, it's the only way to get into the Stasis."

"How did you survive your graduation?" She turned and looked at him, her eyes glistening with unshed tears. "You can be very slow at times, Pierce."

"What—"

"You don't have to abide by what they made you do, my love. Corrupt practices, the use of complicity in shared atrocities to bind new recruits to a cause: it was a late addition to the training protocol, added at the request of Internal Affairs. It may even be what sparked the first muttering of Opposition. We've got the luxury of unmaking our mistakes—even to go back, unmake the mistake, and *not* enter the Stasis, despite having graduated. Agents do that, sometimes, when they're too profoundly burned-out to continue: they go underground, they run and cut themselves off. That's why there was no agent covering the Hegemony period you landed in. They'd erased their history with the Stasis, going into deep cover."

"You say 'they.' Are you by any chance trying to disown their action?" he asked gently.

"No!" *Now* she sounded irritated. "I regret nothing. *She* regrets nothing. Withholding the truth from you for all those years—well, what would you have done if you'd known that your adoring Xiri, the mother of your children, was a deep-cover agent of the Opposition? *What would you have done?*" She reached across and seized his elbow, staring at him, searching for some truth he couldn't articulate.

"I...don't...know." His shoulders slumped.

"All those years, you were under observation by other instances of yourself, sworn in service to Internal Affairs, reporting to Kafka," she pointed out. "Honesty wasn't an option. Not unless you can guarantee that *all* of those ghost-instances would be complicit in keeping the secret, from the moment you were recruited by the Stasis."

"That's why, back in college—" The moment of enlightenment was shocking. Yarrow's mouth, seen for the first time, wide and sensual, the pale lips, his reaction. He looked across the bench, saw the brightness in her eyes as she nodded. "I'd never betray her."

"It happened more than once, according to the Final Library. They can make you betray anyone if they get their claws into you early enough. The only way to prevent it is to make a palimpsest of your whole recruitment into the Stasis—to replace your conscript youth with a disloyal impostor from the outset, or to decline the invitation altogether, and go underground."

"But, I. Him. I'm not him, exactly."

She let go of his elbow. "Not unless you want to be, my love."

"*Am* I your love? Or is he?"

"That depends which version of you you want to be."

"You're telling me that essentially I can only be free of Internal Affairs if I undo what they made me do."

"There's a protocol," she said, looking away. "We can reactivate your phone. You don't have to reenlist in the Stasis if you don't want to. There are berths waiting for all of us on the colony ships…"

"But that's just exchanging one sort of reified destiny for another, isn't it? Expansion in space, instead of time. Why is that any better than, say, freeing the machines, turning over all the available temporal bandwidth to timelike computing to see if the wild-eyed prophets of artificial intelligence and ghosts uploaded in the machines were onto something after all?"

She looked at him oddly. "Do you have any idea how weird you can be at times?"

He snorted. "Don't worry, I'm not serious about that. I know my limits. If I don't do this thing we're discussing, him upstairs will be annoyed. Because Kafka will have all those naively loyal young potential me's to send on spy missions, won't he?" Pierce took a deep breath. "I don't see that there's any *alternative*, really. And that's what rankles. I had hoped that the Opposition would be willing to give me a little more freedom of action than Kafka, that's all." He felt the ghostly touch of a bunch of raisin-wrinkled grape joints holding his preteen wrists, showing him how to cast a line. He owed it to Grandpa, he felt: to leave his own children a universe with elbow room unconstrained by the thumbcuffs of absolute history. "Will you still be here when I get back?"

She regarded him gravely. "Will you still want to see me afterward?"

"Of course."

"See you later, then." She smiled as she stood up, then departed.

He stared at the spot where she'd been sitting for what seemed like a long, long time. But when he tried to remember her face all he could see was the two of them, Xiri and Yarrow, superimposed.

SAYING GOOD-BYE TO NOW

TWENTY YEARS IN STASIS. Numerous deaths, many of them self-inflicted, ordered with the callous detachment of self-appointed gods. They feed into the unquiet conscience of a man who knows he could have been better, can *still* be better—if only he can untangle the Gordian knot of his destiny after it's been tied up and handed to him by people he's coming to despise.

That's you in a nutshell, Pierce.

You're at a bleak crossroads, surrounded by lovers and allies and oh, so isolated in your moment of destiny. Who are you going to be, really? Who do you *want* to be?

All the myriad ways will lie before you, all the roads not taken at your back: who do *you* want to be?

You have met your elder self, the man-machine at the center of an intrigue that might never exist if Kafka gets his way. And you'll have mapped out the scope of the rift with Xiri, itself rooted in her despair at Stasis. You can examine your life with merciless, refreshing clarity, and find it wanting if you wish. You can even unmake your mistakes: let Grandpa flower, prune back your frightened teenage nightmare of murder. You can step off the murderous infinite roundabout whenever you please, resign the game or rejoin and play to win—but the question you've only recently begun to ask is, who writes the rules?

Who do you want to *be*?

The snow falls silently around you as you stand in darkness, knee-deep in the frosted weeds lining the ditch by the railroad tracks. Alone in the night, a young man walks between islands of light. A headhunter stalks him unseen, another young man with a heart full of fears and ears stuffed with lies. There's a knife in his sleeve and a pebble-sized machine in his pocket, and you know what he means to do, and what will come of it. And you know what *you* need to do.

And now it's your turn to start making history...